The
Hong Kong-Zhuhai-Macao
Bridge

新世界出版社
NEW WORLD PRESS

First Edition 2019

By *The Hong Kong-Zhuhai-Macao Bridge* Production Team
Book Design by He Yuting
Layout Design by Wei Fangfang
Copyright by New World Press, Beijing, China

ISBN 978-7-5104-6682-3

Published by
NEW WORLD PRESS
24 Baiwanzhuang Street, Beijing 100037, China

Distributed by
NEW WORLD PRESS
24 Baiwanzhuang Street, Beijing 100037, China
Tel: 86-10-68995968
Fax: 86-10-68998705
Website: www.nwp.com.cn
E-mail: nwpcd@sina.com

Printed in the People's Republic of China

Contents

Preface

Hong Kong-Zhuhai-Macao Bridge — an Awesome Documentary!

Chen Guangzhong

In the 1950s, I had the privilege of taking part in the filming of the documentary movie *Wuhan Yangtze River Bridge* and becoming a witness to history. We live in a great era during which a large number of world-class construction projects have been built. Yan Dong and his team filmed pretty much the entire construction process of the Hong Kong-Zhuhai-Macao Bridge (the Bridge), one of China's major projects in the new century, depicting enumerable diligent, wise and courageous builders. As the completed documentary *The Hong Kong-Zhuhai-Macao Bridge* (*The Bridge*) is published as a book by New World Press, I am happy to take this opportunity to give a few comments on the movie.

1. Straightforward narration – the spirit of documentary value

China has undergone unprecedented change in the past 40 years beginning with the initiation of reform and opening up to the outside world. Never before has technology changed our minds, ideas and the status of our living the way it has today. The turn of events and almost all information of the world can be accessed through the screens of pocket-size smartphones and tablets. In no other era have humans felt more keenly how closely tied they are to each other in their common destiny, in no other era has the world paid so much and so concentrated attention to China, and in no other era have we Chinese been so confident about and so close to fulfilling our great goal of national rejuvenation.

That's the kind of historical background in which *The Hong Kong-Zhuhai-Macao Bridge*, a premium CCTV production, premiered with quite a sensation. The eye-opening Bridge marks the first co-built cross-sea transport project under the "one country, two systems" framework. It is the world's longest cross-sea steel-structure bridge with the world's longest underwater tunnel system.

The Hong Kong-Zhuhai-Macao Bridge has pushed the boundaries of possibility in a spirit of self-reliance and innovation, filled a number of technology gaps, set a bunch of world records, showed China's strength, and gave the world another surprise. In 2015, *The Guardian* referred to it as one of the "Seven Wonders of the Modern World."

Though thoughts had been given to come up with a more appealing, powerful and marketable title for the documentary, the author eventually decided that the Bridge itself actually speaks louder than anything else. The Bridge is a business card of its own. Any effort to make it look better is equivalent to trying to improve the perfect.

The Hong Kong-Zhuhai-Macao Bridge is a straightforward title, clear and simple, reflecting both the Bridge's uniqueness, originality and irreplaceable authority and the very essence of the factual nature of documentaries. In their pursuit of truth, beauty, originality and depth, Director Yan Dong and his team have displayed a sincere artistic character marked by burning passion and cool reason. The documentary is a song of China's path of peace and development and a story about the Bridge told to the world from the starting point of a new era, the vantage point of a community of shared future, and in the spotlight of growing global competition.

2. Hardship-driven momentum and creativity

The movie is a true picture of the hardships, challenges and risks that the Bridge has witnessed during the process of construction. To put that in context, Chinese engineers on study tours abroad were turned down when they simply requested to take a look at a gravel leveling ship, and when seeking counsel on specific technological issues, they met with quotes of 1.5 billion yuan for technology transfer. As a result, the engineers returned to China empty-handed. However, Chinese engineers did not let disappointment kill their hope. Instead, they became more determined and more geared-up toward their goal and finally made breakthroughs in the high-tech arena. Indeed, the Bridge itself is a series of stories of conflict and tension and twists and turns that were unknown to the public before the premiering of the documentary.

3. The power of true stories

What makes *The Hong Kong-Zhuhai-Macao Bridge* stand out is that, different from traditional documentaries, it converts the communication value of a "super project" documentary into a movie of artistic appeal, penetrating thought, and spiritual radiance. A good story is inseparable from real people, real events, real feelings, real words and truth itself. Facts speak louder than words – that's the banner of *The Hong Kong-Zhuhai-Macao Bridge*! Rejecting fancy format or scene reproduction, the movie demonstrates soft and hard power through the use of true facts. By letting facts speak, the movie skips all unnecessary empty words and goes straight to the miracle done through the steadfast spirit of hard work, thus creating a powerful impact on the audience.

4. Giving life to an inanimate structure

A bridge is a means of transport used to overcome a barrier and cut travel time. The Hong Kong-Zhuhai-Macao Bridge, however, is more than a connection between three geographical regions. Its strategic, political, economic, and cultural dimensions make it an eye-catcher of the world. Rather than yoked in the trite conventions of a regular and matter-of-fact chronicle of events in a big and all-encompassing way, the movie highlights the key elements, focuses on the hot components, and casts light on the power points. It truthfully portrays the three major components of the project: bridge, island and tunnel, and highlights the unprecedented challenges and difficulties involved with the building of the underwater tunnel. In a colorful way, the movie converts what is technical into something humanistic and transforms through contrast and comparison statistical data into something concrete and perceivable, thus giving us eye-opening food for thought. Steel bars weighing 330,000 tons and reinforced concrete weighing more than 2 million tons used for the 32 immersed tubes would be enough to build eight 828-meter-tall Khalifa Towers. The Bridge is not just an average public transit project, it has a service life of 120 years; nor is it just a high-tech project composed of steel bars, gravel and concrete, but is also mixed and saturated with the bridge-builders' passion, sweat and wisdom. It has a life of its own. Yan Dong and his team touch our emotional pulses with the spirit and soul of the nation, show us the history and fate of the country and of its bridges, and give us pictures of the tradition and development of China's bridge culture through presentation of a variety of bridges, however big or small. Narrating from a humanistic, emotional, real-life and detail-oriented perspective, the movie fills the audience with a sense of warmth and pride.

Through montage of analogies, extension, combination and connection, the documentary expands the theme and lets the audience see China's outreach to the world, the converging of history and current reality, and the spiritual dialogue between the new era and the people today. In addition, through the tracking of, inquiries into and recollections of real people, events and facts, the movie has managed to dig and sift out soul-searching and profoundly touching stories – stories of a documentary nature told effectively and artistically as a result of keen observation, sharp analysis, and swift capture. Facts often have progressive shock and awe effects on people, and suspense and climax typically come on the heels of factual development. In the movie, we see the pairing of science and art, people and emotions, characters and stories, and imagery and thought.

5. A shocking opening

The documentary presents a gorgeous multi-angle aerial view of the Bridge. In the play of radiant sunlight and white clouds, the Bridge seems to be leaping out of the water like a long dragon – magical, beautiful, and intoxicating. Underwater views of the placement and joining of the immersed tubes are no less fascinating. The shocking opening foretells the screening of a breath-taking story.

Just 50 days after it was linked up, the Hong Kong-Zhuhai-Macao

Bridge was hit successively by Super Typhoons Hato and Paka. The storms carved destructive paths in the stricken areas, causing severe damages of different degrees. People were beginning to worry if the Bridge would survive. It did and stayed intact.

6. Traveling in time

The Hong Kong-Zhuhai-Macao Bridge travels in time and connects the past, present and future.

China's modern bridge history started in the flames of war 80 years ago.

Mao Yisheng, known as "the Father of Chinese Bridges," built China's first dual-purpose road-and-railway bridge in 1937, when he was 39 years old. His success dealt a crushing blow to foreign assertions that no Chinese could build a bridge over Qiantang River and no bridge could ever be built in that location at all. However, he had to personally bomb up the bridge in order to prevent Japanese invaders from heading south from northern Zhejiang Province. After the founding of the People's Republic of China, however, larger bridges began to show up in the country.

In 1957, Mao Zedong expressed in a poem his excitement over the completion of the Wuhan Yangtze River Bridge, the first bridge over the Yangtze, after swimming in the river. One couplet of his poem read: "A bridge spans north and south, turning a natural chasm into a thoroughfare." In 1993, as 89-year-old Deng Xiaoping stood on Yangpu Bridge over Huangpu River in Shanghai, he happily wrote the following words: "The road before me enlightens me more than a hundred years' schooling." Historic scenes like these can easily trigger mixed feelings from the audience.

The movie then shifts back to 1954, a year when the Yingtan-Xiamen Railway was built to connect the mainland with Xiamen Island in Fujian Province. Clips of the documentary *Removing Mountains and Filling up the Sea* show barefoot workers standing in shaky wooden boats as one after another they cast huge rocks deep down into the sea. Their statuesque poses inspire awe. Next, the scene switches to the real-life construction site of the artificial island, a component of the Hong Kong-Zhuhai-Macao Bridge. With the help of powerful machines, 120 steel cylinders, each with a height equivalent to a 20-storied building, were implanted at the bottom of the sea before being filled up with sand and turned quickly into a huge artificial island the size of an aircraft-carrier.

The stark contrast between primitive manual labor and modern means of construction is very uplifting as the audience considers what the country has been through. The cuts of scenes across time and space technically adds to the aesthetic appeal of the documentary. The intrinsic logic and rhythm of the movie feature the flow of ethical character, patriotism, and national spirit. The movie presents a cross-country view of the more than a million bridges across rivers, lakes, mountains, plains, cities and villages. Indeed, China has become a world champion in terms of number of bridges. The camera unfolds images of prosperity and compares life in the Guangdong-Hong Kong-Macao Greater Bay Area with life in the greater New York Bay Area, which greatly adds to the fun of watching. Since the launching of reform and opening up, China has made breathtaking progress in bridge-building technology and has made a transition from being a follower to a leader. The movie tells us matter-of-factly that "China speed" has been made possible by generations of Chinese bridge builders who have kept working hard and pressing ahead steadily.

7. Looking for good stories

The documentary truthfully portrays the power of scale, momentum, huge labor force and heavy-duty equipment involved with the Bridge, and captures details such as the positioning and fastening of screws and the quality of welding. The artistic combination of the macroscopic and microscopic lens gives rise to a powerful visual contrast and produces spiritual synchronization and resonance. Rather than stopping at the showing of "muscles," the movie seeks to penetrate into the spiritual world of the builders. While external beauty can please temporarily and give momentary pleasure, only inner beauty can stir up human emotions and dwell permanently in a person's mind. As a non-fictional documentary, it is not hard to present real events as they are. The real challenge is characterization of real and memorable people of individuality. The appeal of *The Bridge* is in the characters, and the characters and *The Bridge* are one. The documentary highlights Lin Ming, chief engineer of the island and tunnel project.

For eight years, Lin and his team labored continuously at Lingding

Sea defying storms, tidal waves, fog and undercurrents over and from the sea. The camera captures in real time Lin's gray hair, tall figure, tired looks, whether in the canteen, during meetings, on the tunnel construction site, on his way back from a failed operation, and while walking back and forth on the shore trying to figure out solutions.... The footage captured truthfully his momentary facial expressions, action and spiritual conditions. The use of location recording provides access to Lin's changing states of mind and lets the audience hear true monologues from his heart. The weight of his burden, bitterness, confidence, anxiety and peace of mind are all written on his face.

Lin took over the project 12 years ago, when he was 48. Long-term exposure to bridge-related work cast in him the courage to take on challenges and the patience and power to crack hard nuts. He is known for his steady state of mind and a good sense of humor. "I walk the tightrope every day, and I'm very nervous about it," he said, "because placement of each of the 33 immersed tubes represents a new start that keeps me on tenterhooks." Immersed tube E15 was finally installed 40 meters underwater after going through three failed operations and 50 hours of sleepless work.

When news of the success came, Lin and his colleagues did not hug or congratulate each other, nor did they even clap their hands. Instead, they fell asleep on desks, on the deck, near the ship staircase, or any spot they could find. In other words, they simply passed out.

8. Setting the right tone

The keynote of *The Hong Kong-Zhuhai-Macao Bridge* is confidence, pride, self-respect and self-improvement. Complacency, arrogance or bragging have no place in it. We must face the world with sobriety. We are a peacefully emerging major power of potential and strength, but not yet a strong power. We must soberly face risks of a changing world and keep strengthening ourselves. The documentary kindles the flames of patriotism within us with real stories and reminds us of the blood-stained truth that backwardness leaves a country vulnerable to attack. Ours is not a time to sleep or celebrate and entertain with songs and dances, ours is a time of trailblazing and hard work and a time to rise to the occasion.

The Hong Kong-Zhuhai-Macao Bridge belongs to both China and

the world. It's a bridge of common destiny transcending ideology and serving as a link between humanity and nature, across all cultures and economies, and is a win-win bridge of peace and development possessed by all, shared by all and enjoyed by all. The documentary is a movie of quality and taste well worth watching because of its excellent theme and rich, inspiring, and thought-provoking content. I hope our young people will get a sense of what is memorable, admirable, adorable and worthy of pursuit after watching it!

A section of the Hong Kong-Zhuhai-Macao Bridge
in construction

Documentary

The Hong Kong-Zhuhai-Macao Bridge

(Part 1)

As China's economy develops, the country's engineers are redefining what infrastructure development means in the 21st century. The latest evidence of this is the Hong Kong-Zhuhai-Macao Bridge. The longest cross-sea bridge in the world, it's designed to last for 120 years.

It will also serve as a symbol of the close links forged under China's "one country, two systems" policy.

SU QUANKE, Chief Engineer, Hong Kong-Zhuhai-Macao Bridge Authority

It's more than just a physical link. It connects our thoughts, our sentiments and the good things we've created together over the years.

This bridge, one of the most advanced infrastructure projects the world has ever seen, was inspired by ancient Chinese bridge-building technology.

MENG FANCHAO, Chief Designer, Section DB01, Hong Kong-Zhuhai-Macao Bridge

Our ancestors built bridges over the Yangtze and Yellow Rivers, using technology unknown in the West at the time.

The more massive the project, the greater the technological challenges.

JING QIANG, Vice Director, Engineering Management Department, Hong Kong-Zhuhai-Macao Bridge Authority

At the bridge design stage, China hadn't yet adopted the relevant stainless steel standard. So we applied the British standard.

With every new achievement, China's engineers have gained in confidence.

LIN MING, Chief Tunnel Engineer, Hong Kong-Zhuhai-Macao Bridge

It's unique. It's a new approach, a new way of thinking.

The Qingzhou shipping channel bridge of the Hong Kong-Zhuhai-Macao Bridge

General Plan of the Hong Kong-Zhuhai-Macao Bridge

In 2009, work began on what would be the world's longest cross-sea bridge. Spanning the Lingding Sea in the Pearl River Delta, it would extend for a total of 55 kilometers. The structure would comprise 22.9 kilometers of steel bridges, four man-made islands and the world's longest submerged sea tunnel – extending for 6.7 kilometers at a depth of 40 meters.

JING QIANG

JING QIANG, Vice Director, Engineering Management Department, Hong Kong-Zhuhai-Macao Bridge Authority

When we chose the design, we still lacked the right technology and equipment. Nobody had attempted anything like it before. The bridge behind me was built in segments. The tower was built at a factory and moved here. It may sound easy now, but eight years ago we didn't have either the technology or the equipment to do it.

Assembly of bottom plates of a box girder

The main body of the Hong Kong-Zhuhai-Macao Bridge is formed of 2,156 box girders, amounting to 400,000 tons of steel – roughly the weight of 60 Eiffel Towers. The girders, each of which measures 132.6 meters, were assembled at Zhongshan in Guangdong and shipped the 40 kilometers to the construction site.

JING QIANG

We're inside a box girder. The assembly has been completed. Once any faults are rectified it'll be painted. We're finishing the undercoat. It's already been inspected. I'll do the final check.

This is the main assembly yard. This is being polished, you see? Here the plate components are joined to make the box shape. We do it one piece at a time. We weld them together into one big piece – a whole segment.

Assembly of top plates of a box girder

Assembly of the box girder has been completed

Inside a box girder

Shipping the first box girder

We conduct full life-cycle monitoring. From the individual plates to the complete segments we monitor the entire process. The segments are kept in storage until they're ready to be sent to the bridge.

Construction of the huge box girder

The Hong Kong-Zhuhai-Macao Bridge is designed to withstand force 16 typhoons and force eight earthquakes. Another principal requirement is that it must not disrupt shipping in the area or flights in and out of Hong Kong and Macao international airports.

Meeting these demands has created the need for a series of innovations in the bridge's design, and in the construction materials and methods. Further

Mounting the first box girder of the CB04 Section

Construction of the huge box girder

breakthroughs will also help ensure that the bridge achieves its planned lifespan of 120 years – a significant advance on the 100 years that large-scale bridges have been designed to last, up until now.

A plan to build a bridge across the Lingding Sea was first discussed in 1983. But to today's engineers, the project is about much more than just realizing an old dream.

The "silver thread" connecting "pearls"

MENG FANCHAO

MENG FANCHAO, Chief Designer, Section DB01, Hong Kong-Zhuhai-Macao Bridge

There's more to this bridge than being a communication channel. On a higher level it has a cultural mission. The bridge spans "one country, two systems" – something unique.There are international bridges but one that spans "one country, two systems" and three regions is the first in the world. The bridge, islands and tunnels give it additional significance as a link across the Pearl River Delta.

SU QUANKE

SU QUANKE, Chief Engineer, Hong Kong-Zhuhai-Macao Bridge Authority

Starting in Zhuhai there are four tunnels, four man-made islands and 40 kilometers of bridges. It's like a silver thread holding together a string of pearls.

"Holding together a string of pearls," this poetic analogy has its origins in the traditional Chinese concept of "stringing pearls and jade

Mounting box girders

Pier placement

together." It describes the close ties between Hong Kong, Macao and the Chinese mainland.

As a symbol of "one country, two systems," the Hong Kong-Zhuhai-Macao Bridge embodies great hopes. When construction began in December 2012, the builders were fully aware that they were facing a huge challenge.

The main part of the project, the 22.9-kilometer-long bridge section over the sea, would need to have the longest possible spans so that it would not impede shipping. The structure would also have to be light, to withstand earthquakes. This made a regular concrete bridge design unsuitable. Instead, the choice fell on a lighter, more durable steel structure.

But this raised another problem. The corrosive effects of the ocean currents could cause serious damage to the bridge's piers, if they were made of steel. The engineers would have to find a type of steel capable of resisting the seawater.

Their search took them to China's most advanced stainless steel plant in the north of the country.

JING QIANG, Vice Director, Engineering Management Department, Hong Kong-Zhuhai-Macao Bridge Authority

This is Tisco, our stainless steel manufacturer. I'm here for three reasons. First, to check on production. Second, to confirm that the finished steel meets our standard. Third, when the bridge is finished, to establish a set of national standards. We're conducting research here and I'm also checking on that.

Taiyuan Iron and Steel – Tisco for short – was the first company in China to produce stainless steel. It has subsequently developed into a leader in the industry, with a current capacity to turn out 12 million tons of steel annually. This includes 4.5 million tons of stainless steel. Even so, supplying all the steel needed for the cross-sea bridge would be a major challenge.

CHAI ZHIYONG

CHAI ZHIYONG, Vice President, Tisco

The specifications are extremely strict. It's a new product, and nothing on this scale has ever been attempted before. Moreover, new standards are being applied. No national standards for it exist yet. We have to adopt an international standard, in this case, the British standard.

Tisco's independent research and development of non-corrosive steel bar

Stainless steel may be corrosion-resistant, but the sea, with its low oxygen and high salt content, still presents an extremely hostile environment. The engineers decided that the best solution might be the stronger, duplex stainless steel. Importing it was ruled out as an option, as the cost was prohibitive.

Tisco rose to the challenge. The company developed its own duplex stainless steel, and committed itself to producing the 8,200 tons needed for the bridge's base, towers and piers.

JING QIANG

It took a 40-ton weight to break this bar. That's the weight of more than 20 sedan cars.

In order to verify the quality of the new steel, Tisco sent it abroad for testing. The product passed with flying colors, and was awarded international certification.

CHAI ZHIYONG

We've had a sound research capability for a while. But since China's shift from a planned to a market economy we've had to produce to order, and nothing else.

The engineering breakthroughs associated with the bridge are not limited to the steel. More than 1,000 patents have been awarded for innovations related to the construction of the bridge, the man-made islands and the tunnels.

MENG FANCHAO, Chief Designer, Section DB01, Hong Kong-Zhuhai-Macao Bridge

Our ultimate aim is to achieve a higher standard than any other cross-sea bridge in China. We're making advances, based on our experience from previous projects – the successful experience and technologies. The technologies are mature but they can still be improved.

The last steel tube for the east man-made island ready to be hammered down

The benefits of the innovations have extended beyond the field of engineering.

SU QUANKE, Chief Engineer, Hong Kong-Zhuhai-Macao Bridge Authority

From here we can see that the bridge bends. It runs from Zhuhai and Macao to Hong Kong – that's a given. But why can't it be straight? It'd be shorter, right? It's because of the shipping lanes, which need to follow the sea currents. Unlike a river, sea currents are changeable. The bridge needs to bend to create a straight angle with the currents. That's why we get this bend. Still, it's quite attractive.

The Hong Kong-Zhuhai-Macao Bridge may be at the forefront of a new generation of modern Chinese bridges. But it's deeply rooted in Chinese bridge-building tradition.

The ancient Chinese were some of the earliest and most prolific bridge-builders in the world. This is hardly surprising, since the country's territory is marked by thousands of crisscrossing rivers. Even in the most remote village, evidence can be found of ancient bridges, built using local materials and know-how.

Why does the bridge bend?

Scene of the bridge

SU QUANKE

Bridges in China, on top of the basic engineering, incorporate a lot of art and are imbued with meaning. In every bridge they build the Chinese instill cultural connotations.

Guangji Bridge is one of the four most celebrated ancient bridges in China. It lies 500 kilometers away from the Hong Kong-Zhuhai-Macao Bridge. Built during the Southern Song Dynasty in the 12th century, it was the first-ever bridge capable of opening to allow ships to pass. It was a key link on the trade routes connecting Guangdong with Fujian, Jiangxi, Zhejiang and other areas to the north and east. Its beauty testifies to the remarkable skill of its builders.

Guangji Bridge (built in 1170 AD), Guangdong Province, China

Haoshang Bridge in Leshan, Sichuan Province, China

MENG FANCHAO, Chief Designer, Section DB01, Hong Kong-Zhuhai-Macao Bridge

It's a well-preserved Chinese bridge, yet it's not suitable as a blueprint for a modern project. Development has to be our constant pursuit.

The Hong Kong-Zhuhai-Macao Bridge project has naturally attracted considerable attention, locally.

CHEN ZHILIANG

LI JIANBIN

CHEN ZHILIANG, Macao Logistics Association

When the bridge opens, it'll take 30 minutes to get from Hong Kong to Macao.

LI JIANBIN, Vice President, Zhuhai High Speed Passenger Ferry Co.

It'll give a boost to the Zhuhai region and the western side of the Pearl River Delta.

ZHANG CHI

FANG SHUYU

ZHANG CHI, Zhuhai Real Estate Agent

When the bridge opens to traffic, it will give a major boost to the Zhuhai real estate market.

FANG SHUYU, Cross-strait Commuter

As for the environment, I don't know whether it may affect the animals living in the ocean.

Chinese white dolphins

In fact, environmental protection has been a major consideration throughout the project. One species in particular has been the subject of concern.

Four adults and three young. See! Three mother-and-young pairs. And one on its own.

The Lingding Sea is home to an estimated 2,000 Chinese white dolphins. The area was designated a dolphin sanctuary in 2003. When it was revealed that the bridge would cut straight across it, there was an initial public outcry.

An investigation was ordered, which concluded that the bridge would indeed affect the local marine wildlife. The bridge authority decided that steps would have to be taken to reduce the impact. So guidelines were published, detailing what should be done at every step of the construction process, to minimize the environmental impact.

The bridge and the Chinese white dolphins

SU QUANKE, Chief Engineer, Hong Kong-Zhuhai-Macao Bridge Authority

We investigated this national dolphin sanctuary. The use of diesel pile hammers was banned, as was dredging the seabed. There could be no pollution or shocks.

A team was appointed, reporting directly to the bridge authority, to oversee implementation of these measures.

HUANG ZHIXIONG, Safety & Environmental Protection Department Hong Kong-Zhuhai-Macao Bridge Authority

HUANG ZHIXIONG

We're monitoring the entire sanctuary. We're also keeping an eye on the project's progress, to make sure that the measures to protect the area are implemented. On a daily basis, we monitor the impact each step in the project has on the dolphins. We need the data in order to protect and manage the area properly.

But the team initially faced an even bigger challenge, which is to change people's stereotpyes.

WEN HUA, Safety & Environmental Protection Department Hong Kong-Zhuhai-Macao Bridge Authority

When we first inspected the site many of the workers told us, "We get it, but it's what they do abroad." We spent a lot of time explaining to them that this is a sanctuary and certain things were important.

The groundbreaking work done by the environmental protection team will provide a model for future infrastructure projects in China.

WEN HUA

HUANG ZHIXIONG, Safety & Environmental Protection Department Hong Kong-Zhuhai-Macao Bridge Authority

It's a process. Panda protection also had to be promoted by the government and a lot of work had to be done before any results were seen. There's a lack of research.

In China at the moment we have to build things in order to develop the economy. But by also learning from experience abroad we can gradually change attitudes and work practices. If we invest greater efforts and resources, I think we can do this.

Creating awareness is only one of the measures the builders are taking to tackle with the issue of environmental sustainability.

The environmental protection team of the bridge

The Lingding Sea is prone to frequent typhoons. For almost 200 days of every year, it's subjected to winds in excess of 50 meters per second. With 4,000 ships using the channel every day, the engineers are confronted by a major challenge.

An airplane flying over the construction site

But that's not all. Flights to and from the nearby Hong Kong International Airport are constantly using the airspace here. To avoid the possibility of accidents, the height to which any part of the bridge may rise, was severely restricted. This raises the question of whether it's worth pouring such massive investment into such a complex project. To answer it, one needs to look abroad.

New York City, with its 8.5 million inhabitants, is the most densely populated metropolis in the United States. Much like the Pearl River Delta, rivers divide the city into five administrative districts. One of New York's annual bicycle races illustrates how easy it is to cross the boundaries between them.

Bicycle Racers

Yes I am living here for six years already, and the bridges are a very important part of New York City as a whole.

A bicycle racer

Bicycle racers

I mean you stand down below and you look up at the sky and see them against the horizon, and they're beautiful.

Including its waters, New York covers roughly 1,200 square kilometers. In this area some 2,000 bridges, big and small, have been built. They are the threads weaving the city into a whole.

VICKEN VARIAN

VICKEN VARIAN, Project Executive, China Construction America Civil

New York is three big islands. You have Long Island which has Manhattan, Queens and Brooklyn. And then you have Staten Island. The only part of New York that is not an island is Bronx. So just to connect these islands together you need a lot of bridges.

CHARLES MONTALLBANO

CHARLES MONTALLBANO, President, China Construction America Civil

It's constantly growing and adding and we need to keep up with the infrastructure to keep up with that growth. And it's important for the economic vitality of this area.

PETER WU

PETER WU, Vice President, China Construction America

Now we're building a very very large bridge to connect Hong Kong, Macao and the Chinese mainland. I definitely believe that this magnificent bridge, upon completion, will not only drive the economy of those three places but also definitely change the lifestyle of the people. The bridge is changing the culture.

New York City became New York City today because of those bridges. This is one of the reasons, because those bridges connect the whole city and move the people. And each bridge has its own story.

WEI DONGQING, Administrative Director, Hong Kong-Zhuhai-Macao Bridge Authority

Over 60 million people live in the Pearl River Delta area. It's China's most developed region. As the first place to open up to the world it's the cradle of modern Chinese thinking. Modern Chinese history begins beside the Lingding Sea.

The west side of the Pearl River Delta has always dreamed of being connected to the east.

WEI DONGQING

CHEN GUANGHAN, Director, Centre for Hong Kong, Macao and Pearl River Delta Studies

Historically, this region was China's gateway to the world. The Pearl River Delta focused on trade. That's why Deng Xiaoping made it a special economic zone.

CHEN GUANGHAN

The eastern part of the Pearl River Delta is developing faster. Hong Kong is a key factor in this. Investment, capital and business radiate from Hong Kong, driving development on the east side. So Zhuhai and the surrounding area on the west have always wanted a connection to Hong Kong.

Economists have high hopes for the Hong Kong-Zhuhai-Macao Bridge. The bridge will tie the three cities closer together, and boost development in the Guangdong-Hong Kong-Macao area. But how will the bridge change the life of the people living in the area, most of whom currently rely on the ferry to cross the strait?

LI JIANBIN, Vice President, Zhuhai High Speed Passenger Ferry Co.

When the bridge opens it'll take away part of our business. Some of our customers will use the bridge. But it's a huge project. It'll boost the economy of the entire Pearl River Delta region.

When planning was underway for the bridge we analyzed the situation and adjusted our company's strategy. We'll adapt to the new era of the bridge. We'll change and upgrade and focus more on marine tourism.

While people in Zhuhai are clearly keen for the bridge to open, what about those in Macao?

CHEN ZHILIANG, Macao Logistics Association

Macao imports most of its daily necessities from Hong Kong. Some come from abroad via the airport. We're dependent on Hong Kong for shipping, which takes a day. Once the bridge opens it'll take 30 minutes. So urgent shipments of food, frozen goods and e-commerce related goods can get here faster.

SHI JIALUN

SHI JIALUN, Macao Legislator

In Macao's 2016 policy statement we suggested creating a special financial platform. How would we do that? By relying on mainland businesses. How could they come here? How could we attract them? I think the Hong Kong-Zhuhai-Macao Bridge will be a key factor and will be good for Macao.

The Qingzhou shipping channel bridge of the Hong Kong-Zhuhai-Macao Bridge

The Pearl River Delta accounts for just 1% of China's land area, but contributes more than one tenth of its GDP. With this in mind, the fact that the Hong Kong-Zhuhai-Macao Bridge will cut straight across the region's profitable shipping lanes, has raised some concerns.

To alleviate these worries, the bridge's several spans are designed so that existing shipping routes are not compromised. The engineers are also breaking new ground by designing an ocean tunnel, 6.7 kilometers long. At its lowest, the tunnel will pass 40 meters below the surface. This is deep enough for ships of up to 300,000 tons to pass over.

Will the bridge have impact upon the Lingding Sea?

The bridge's multi-shipping channel design

But with no precedent to refer to, the engineers would have to develop brand-new techniques for getting the job done.

Lin Ming is the tunnel's chief engineer. He is a veteran of numerous major projects. But this is an unprecedented challenge, even for him.

LIN MING

LIN MING, Chief Tunnel Engineer

We've been working very hard for many years. Now this is the last piece. The section is 180m long. It's the last one.

Outfitting tunnel section E1

The first tunnel section in production

The ocean tunnel comprises 33 sections, each 180 meters long. Installation began in 2013. Each section must be sunk with pinpoint accuracy. But the Lingding Sea's unpredictable tides and waves have made the work very dangerous. Even so, in less than 48 hours' time, Lin Ming and his team will lower the last one into position.

Lin Ming has brought out the biggest gun in his arsenal – a platform specially designed for the project.

This platform represents another major achievement for Chinese engineering.

LIN MING

The Koreans had one of these which they'd imported from Europe.
We got ZMPC to do some research and they built this platform for the project.

Outdocking a tunnel section

Send it on WeChat!
Did you take a picture? Take one!
Then come with me.

We use our own intelligence to solve problems while relying on global resources.

In building this huge bridge, the number of technical innovations was more than most engineers could hope to see in a lifetime.

SU QUANKE, Chief Engineer, Hong Kong-Zhuhai-Macao Bridge Authority

When we were first told about the bridge across the Lingding Sea it sounded impossible. It's an ocean! We don't have the technology to span it!

Our leaders said: The need is there and we can learn the techniques from abroad. We can import them or learn them. But we'll build a few other bridges first.

I said: Sounds good. Let's start practicing.

In 1991, I applied to take part in the Shantou Bay Bridge project.

It was a long way away, but I wanted to go.

My boss said: Good, go and practice. Get ready for the Lingding Sea Bridge. Then we built several cross-sea bridges.

Humen Bridge in Guangdong Province (Opened in 1997)

By this time, bridge-builders all across China were honing their skills.

MENG FANCHAO, Chief Designer, Section DB01, Hong Kong-Zhuhai-Macao Bridge

Back then, we relied mainly on small machinery and manpower to get things done. I remember at the work site the old workers and engineers would tell us how they'd use leftover tools. Machines, tools and skills... Also, they had Soviet help. Back then a lot of China's technology imports, including materials and equipment, came from the Soviet Union.

After 1949, Soviet technology played a key role in China's infrastructure development. Completed in 1957, the Yangtze River Bridge in Wuhan, the first-ever bridge built over the Yangtze, was a fruit of Soviet aid. It was also the first bridge over the Yangtze to carry both road and rail transport. As the final link in the Beijing to Guangzhou railway – a major north-south artery – the bridge overcame one of the biggest natural barriers in China. Old footage shows the elation of the people who witnessed the opening of this historic bridge.

Celebration for the opening of the Yangtze River Bridge in Wuhan (1957)

Celebration for the opening of the Yangtze River Bridge in Nanjing (1968)

Puli Bridge in Yunnan Province (opened in 2015)

Longjiang Bridge in Yunnan Province (opened in 2016)

MENG FANCHAO, Chief Designer, Section DB01, Hong Kong-Zhuhai-Macao Bridge

The Hong Kong-Zhuhai-Macao Bridge is based on four concepts: scale, factory production, standardization and assembly.

The precast plant of tunnel sections

What changes will the breakthroughs in technology and standards bring to the bridge-building industry?

Back in 1894, the Shanhaiguan Bridge Factory, the predecessor of the China Railway Shanhaiguan Bridge Group, was already building modern bridges.

LI HUICHENG

The welding robot developed by China Railway Shanhaiguan Bridge Group

LI HUICHENG, General Manager, China Railway Shanhaiguan Bridge Group

The company was set up to build bridges. When it built its first bridge, it was the British who made the sections, and these were assembled in Shanhaiguan.

For the Hong Kong-Zhuhai-Macao Bridge we've mobilized the entire company. This bridge is a symbol of China, a centennial project. Our company has a long history. We should take on this mission.

The robots enabled the factory to a complicated work that was beyond the capability of any human worker.

A welding robot at China Railway Shanhaiguan Bridge Group

LI HUICHENG

This workshop covers 165 acres. The entire factory covers 14,000 acres. After finishing this bridge we'll be building seven or eight more. The biggest is Padma Bridge in Bangladesh. This is a huge factory, so we can work on several projects simultaneously.

LIU ENGUO, Supervisory Committee Chairman, China Railway Hi-tech Industry Corp.

LIU ENGUO

I don't think of it as just a bridge or a project. I think of how it will boost our company's technological advances and how it will help us to expand internationally.

In this way China, after developing new capabilities for itself, is sharing them with the rest of the world.

CHEN HONGKE, Temburong Bridge Project

I was born in Sichuan and went to university in 1994. I never thought I'd get to work abroad and benefit people there. The Temburong Cross-sea Bridge will be 30 kilometers long. The project's invested by the government of Brunei. Temburong is separated from the mainland by the Brunei Bay. The bridge will connect them.

CHEN HONGKE

WILLY TEN JYH CHYN, Brunei Department of the Environment

Personally I think doing sustainable engineering is very difficult. Another thing is commitment – whether a company can commit to this sustainable engineering or sustainable construction and spend money to comply with the specifications, which is a good sign. Environmental protection costs money and it doesn't come cheap. Back when I was younger, to be honest, I never thought that a Chinese company will come in and build something so great, so big that change the people's lives here in the future. So obviously as a local I can't wait to finish the bridge on time and people can start

WILLY TEN JYH CHYN

A construction site of the Temburong Bridge

using this facility that the government provided to the population.

In faraway Brunei, the Chinese engineering team is facing a number of challenges to complete the bridge on time. Meanwhile, the engineers at the Pearl River Delta are preparing to put in place the last piece of the puzzle that will form the longest submerged sea tunnel in the world.

LIN MING, Chief Tunnel Engineer

I got up early to go for a jog but I'd forgotten my training pants. So I couldn't.

This is the last one, I keep thinking. I'm worried we've overlooked something. Just a little worried.

From 2013... Through 2014, 2015... More than three years. Now it's the last time. So we've prepared very well. But this time we've only had a fortnight. So we must be careful.

Over the last three years, Lin Ming and his team have installed 32 sections of the tunnel beneath the sea. This is the grand finale. The team is nervous. The smallest mistake could undermine all their hard work to date.

LIN MING

The weather today should be generally good. It's the last one so we're hoping for good weather.

The section is the length of two football pitches. It's the longest tunnel section ever laid under the sea, anywhere in the world. Out on the rough surface, moving the huge section by just one centimeter requires meticulous planning and the power of a small fleet of ships. Twice in the last four years, Lin Ming and his team have had to abort the installation of a section because of a change in the weather. Will the weather gods smile on them this time?

Ready to install the
last tunnel section

The last tunnel section E30

The Lingding Sea

Documentary
The Hong Kong-Zhuhai-Macao Bridge
(Part 2)

This is the Pearl River Delta in southern China. An inspection team is about to get to work, checking the installation of the final section of the longest submerged sea tunnel in the world.

LIAO JIANHUA, Underwater Inspection Team Leader

We're going to check whether this section meets the design specifications. This is the first deep-water submerged sea tunnel in China.

The underwater inspection team was established especially for this project – a project that will redefine the meaning of "Made in China."

The tunnel is part of a brand-new type of bridge, built at a time when China is emerging as a global leader in bridge-building. It's the Hong Kong-Zhuhai-Macao Bridge. Once completed, it will be the longest cross-sea bridge in the world. Built to last for 120 years, it will link Hong Kong, Macao and the Chinese mainland, becoming a symbol of the "one country, two systems" policy.

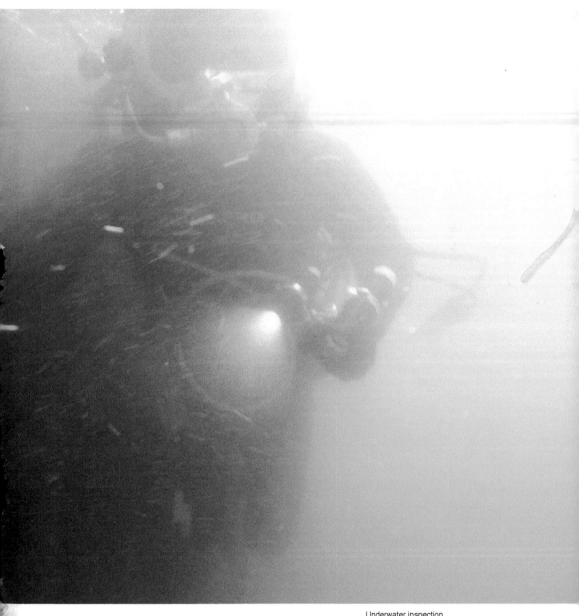

Underwater inspection

A section of the Hong Kong-Zhuhai-Macao Bridge in construction

SU QUANKE, Chief Engineer, Hong Kong-Zhuhai-Macao Bridge Authority

We're building a connection, a link.

Innovation is key to the project's success.

JING QIANG, Vice Director, Engineering Management Department, Hong Kong-Zhuhai-Macao Bridge Authority

When we chose the design, we still lacked the right technology and equipment. Nobody had attempted anything like it before.

What sacrifices were required to make this mega project a reality?

A section of the spectacular Hong Kong-Zhuhai-Macao Bridge in construction

WEN HUA, Safety & Environmental Protection Department, Hong Kong-Zhuhai-Macao Bridge Authority

Some of them haven't been home for years. Their children no longer recognize them.

The project has given birth to a new generation of engineers. What does this bridge mean to them?

LIN MING, Chief Tunnel Engineer

Some of us have worked here from the age of 30 to 40, some from 20 to 30. This project is part of our lives.

For over a decade, engineering teams from every corner of China have been quietly contributing to the Hong Kong-Zhuhai-Macao Bridge.

XIE HONGBING, Engineer

This cooperation between three regional governments is not easy, because we have different systems for project management. Even for the technical specifications, the standards are different. It's a sign for the three regions to be one family. [That's] the target of the project. We want to build a world-class sea-crossing link that can best serve the user and become a landmark.

XIE HONGBING

Major structure of the bridge

With the completion date approaching, engineers are working against the clock to lower the last tunnel section into place, 40 meters below the surface.

The section is the length of two football pitches. It's the longest tunnel section ever laid under the sea, anywhere in the world. Chief engineer Lin Ming and his team are tasked with moving this 80,000-ton

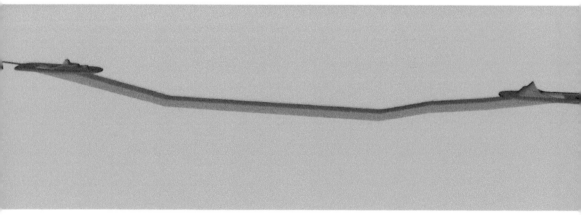

An illustration of the tunnel

The last tunnel section to be placed

giant to its designated position. It's a risky operation, which raises the question: Is this bridge really worth it?

CHEN GUANGHAN, Director, Centre for Hong Kong, Macao and Pearl River Delta Studies

The bridge will bring the two shores into a single circle and draw the delta together. The economic benefits will become clear with time.

The bridge, by spanning the Lingding Sea, will join the biggest cities in the region, creating one vast metropolitan district – the Guangdong-Hong Kong-Macao Greater Bay Area. This area already contributes 10% of China's GDP. The engineers are working flat-out to complete the bridge and make their contribution to boosting urbanization in China.

Moving the tunnel section by just one centimeter requires a whole fleet of ships to work together in unison.

LIN MING, Chief Tunnel Engineer

We've got 13 ships. Four are over here. Another four are there. They're our usual eight. Today, we want to step things up. For the first time, as you can see, we've got two more boats up front. So we can go faster. It's like playing chess.

But Lin Ming is playing a complicated game. On his chess board, 40 ships and almost 300 workers are on the move. Danger lurks at every move. More than 4,000 ships pass through the Lingding Sea daily. To reduce the risk of collision, Guangdong's maritime authority has ordered that the area be cleared.

With all traffic temporarily banished from their route, Lin Ming's team can make their move. They have to transport the section three kilometers off shore. Out at sea, it takes three hours to move the section just 200 meters. Lin Ming is gambling that his more powerful fleet of ships will increase this speed. However, the immense forces involved mean that the slightest false move can cause an accident. A wire may snap, endangering the life of the crew. Fortunately, Lin has years of experience to draw on.

LIN MING

The first time we did this I felt like a first-time driver. I was driving without proper training. We made our own equipment and then started driving. We wanted to hire someone to teach us, but it was too expensive. They wanted over a billion yuan. Without an instructor the pressure was immense. It was very tough, but because we had no one to help us we were able to develop our own methods.

The towing fleet

Lin's innovative approach seems to be a success. With the new ship formation, the tunnel section has covered half the distance at twice the normal speed, but then there's a problem.

Begin to place the last tunnel section

LIN MING

We're waiting for the current to change. We'll turn when it slows. We've got one kilometer still to go. The current's like a red light. It won't let us change direction.

The team face an eight-hour wait. It will be a test of their morale, but it's nothing new to them.

LIN MING

Wait for orders. We're stopping. Wait for us to turn. We'll have to wait for about an hour for the tide to turn.
The plan's unchanged.
We'll attach it tomorrow.

The Anlan Bridge in Sichuan Province, one of China's most famous ancient bridges

Behind every engineering marvel lie the sacrifices of countless people. The Great Wall is a symbol of Chinese civilization and the nation's perseverance in overcoming challenges.

This is Anlan Bridge – part of the Dujiangyan irrigation system in Sichuan – believed to have been built in the third century BC. In the course of over two millennia, it has been destroyed several times in natural and man-made disasters. However, it has always been rebuilt to provide safe passage over the raging river.

SUN HONGCHUN

SUN HONGCHUN, 2nd Island and Tunnel Construction Site

There are 500 people from all over the country. The key areas in China's development lie on the coast. Workers have come here from the hinterland.

The eastern island is the furthest from land. Before we began this was open sea. At first, we lived on boats. We had 200 people on each boat – there was no room to move.

Sun Hongchun and his colleagues have had to make other sacrifices. Sun was introduced to his future wife over the telephone. They married very soon after meeting for the first time.

Before that first meeting, their only contact had been via video calls. His wife is also working on the bridge. But she was assigned to another work site.

SUN HONGCHUN

We don't have a home of our own. When I get time off, I go to her worksite. If we get time off together, we visit our parents. Home is the village we grew up in.

Still, some of the workers have it easier.

WEN HUA, Safety & Environmental Protection Department, Hong Kong-Zhuhai-Macao Bridge Authority

I'm lucky. I'm from Zhuhai, right where the project is. A lot of people are jealous. They'll ask me if I'm going home again to have soup. They're jealous. They haven't been home for years. Their children don't recognize them.

I think it's like this in many places, not just China. Of course, China's a big country, so sometimes it's like this, but they're proud of their work. After all, it's a mega project on a national scale. Of course, they sacrifice a lot.

SUN HONGCHUN

Somebody has to build these things. If we don't, someone else will have to. If other people can manage it, why not me?

Working on this kind of mega project, you somehow get drawn to it. You get this sense of mission.

Every day, over 6 million tons of cargo passes through the Pearl River Delta, on ships that dock in Hong Kong, Shenzhen and Guangzhou. Building a bridge in these busy waters will inevitably have an impact on shipping. The original design envisaged making the bridge high enough for ships to pass under it. However, not all the traffic in the area is on the sea.

A tunnel construction site

Construction of the immersed tunnel

The bridge lies near Hong Kong International Airport. Safety regulations dictated that the bridge's towers could be no taller than 88 meters. So the designers came up with another solution – building part of the bridge under water. Thus, the plan to build a 6.7-kilometer-long submerged sea tunnel was born.

Constructing the tunnel necessitated further technological breakthroughs. The tunnel would be formed of 33 pre-fabricated sections, each of which would be 180 meters long on average and weigh 50,000 tons. The sections were made at a facility on Niutou Island. Once completed, they were sealed and floated to the construction site.

HANS DE WIT, Tunnel Engineering Consultant, TEC

These are by far the biggest immersed tunnel elements that have ever been used. I've been in China since 2008, when they started the project. They started it from scratch, developing the technologies and introducing innovations that were thoroughly tested and studied, and made sure that they could meet the very stringent requirements...

HANS DE WIT

A man-made island in construction

These steel tubes formed the foundation on which the islands were built. Before long, a connection between tunnel and bridge was taking shape.

While on the Zhuhai side the solution was to create new land in the form of islands, in Hong Kong land was reclaimed.

It was originally estimated that building the islands would take over two years, much longer than the schedule allowed. Once again, a creative solution was needed. So the engineers decided to drive enormous steel tubes, 30 meters down into the seabed. In all, 120 tubes were used to form the outline of each of the two islands. Each tube was 22 meters in diameter and 40 to 50 meters tall.

Steel tubes

The last steel tube in the construction of the western man-made island

YU PEIZHONG, Vice President, China Construction Intl (Hong Kong Construction)

I'm a senior regional manager. I've been working on the project for five years. This stretch is 2.65-kilometer-long and comprises a 1.1-kilometer tunnel and 1.5 kilometers of road. The road is built on 23 hectares of reclaimed land. It involved the biggest blasting operation on the island since the airport was built.

YU PEIZHONG

The bridge reaches Hong Kong near the international airport. The unique environment here presented the engineers with a new set of challenges.

The connection is 12 kilometers long. However, this is not one straight road, but comprises a 9.4-kilometer-long bridge, a 1.1-kilometer-long tunnel and 1.5 kilometers of highway linked to Hong Kong port. This complex connection was divided into several sections, which were built simultaneously.

The Hong Kong concept of the connection

XIE XUNYOU, Project Representative

The difficult bit in this project is that we are inside the airport island. So we have the oil fuel tanks over there. On the left-hand side is the cable car transfer station. And in front, we have a light traffic road.

XIE XUNYOU

The Hong Kong connection could not disrupt air traffic to and from the airport; nor could it damage any of the existing infrastructure. The engineers solved this issue by building a new island to use as a transfer point. However, construction was far from easy.

The man-made island in Hong Kong as a transfer point

YU PEIZHONG

The environment was a challenge because we had to reclaim land. We did it without dredging, despite having to reclaim 23 hectares, so we developed some new methods.

Traditionally, reclaiming land involves dredging the sea bed, but this inevitably harms the environment. To avoid this, metal tubes were once again called upon to form a perimeter.

However, the area is surrounded by hills, which complicated the road construction. A 1.1-kilometer-long tunnel would have to be built. By building it in four sections simultaneously, it could be completed in half the normal time.

A tunnel construction site

YU PEIZHONG

It's just over a kilometer long but we used four different methods to build it. One hadn't been used in Hong Kong before. We incrementally added six prefabricated sections. Each one weighed almost 5,000 tons. A maximum thrust of 17,000 tons was required.

For the workers from the mainland, the project offered some unexpected benefits.

YU PEIZHONG

We came to Hong Kong soon after graduating from university. There were differences in language and culture. There was less contact with the mainland then, especially around a decade ago, but with some help from the project and the company, we've adapted to and become integrated into the local culture.

Far away, in New York City, Chinese engineers are working with their American colleagues to maintain and build the city's many bridges. During their stay, they have learned a lot about bridges in America.

VICKEN VARIAN, Project Executive, CCA Civil

This is the Gerritsen Inlet project for CCA. We're constructing a brand-new bridge. The old bridge was built in the late 1930's to the early 40's but has seen very little maintenance. What you see here is all brand-new. We take advantage of the new technology and new material so they should last longer than the old bridges although we have to give credit to the people before us when they built the bridges.

The Gerritsen Inlet project built by CCA

PETER WU, Vice President, China Construction America

New York City became New York City today is because of those bridges. From the late 1800s to the 1950s, US civil engineers created a lot of miracles, including the Brooklyn Bridge, George Washington Bridge, Lincoln Tunnel, Holland Tunnel, Grand Central Terminal and the JFK Airport. And the whole world is still benefiting from those engineering innovations.

But is the West still at the head of the pack when it comes to civil engineering? If so, how long will it remain there?

MENG FANCHAO, Chief Designer, Section DB01, Hong Kong-Zhuhai-Macao Bridge

Prior to the 1970s, where was the global center of bridge building? In Europe and America. From the 1970s to the early 21st century, where was this center then? In Japan. The Japanese, after their economy took off, built some of the world's greatest cross-sea bridges and tunnels. Since the early 21st century, you could say this center is in China.

The Golden Gate Bridge in San Francisco, the United States (opened in 1937)

The Akashi Kaikyō Bridge in Japan (opened in 1998)

Over the last 20 years, China has constructed a huge number of bridges. At first, progress was slow, but it soon took off. This development is part of a grander scheme.

The Hangzhou Bay Bridge in China (opened in 2008)

The Chaotianmen Yangtze River Bridge in Chongqing, China (opened in 2009)

SU QUANKE, Chief Engineer, Hong Kong-Zhuhai-Macao Bridge Authority

The Shantou Bay Bridge in 1991, the Humen Bridge in 1992 and the Haicang Bridge in 1997 – all prepared us for building this bridge.

JING QIANG, Vice Director, Engineering Management Department, Hong Kong-Zhuhai-Macao Bridge Authority

I dreamt of such a bridge when I was at school. Who would have known that my dream would become part of my job – the reality? I'm lucky to be a part of it. I've witnessed the technological advances that it has brought.

When we decided on the plan we didn't have this equipment, and nobody had done anything like it before.

It describes a 180-degree bend but the curve mustn't have any cracks. If it does, it will fail testing. So if you look at this coating, the thicker it is, the more difficult it is to create a bend.

This generation of bridge builders are lucky. The state supports us, the economy is strong, and we have the technology and equipment. We have all of these.

Innovation of construction technologies

Steel bar testing

Engineers, however experienced they may be, have to tread carefully when attempting something that has never been done before. Lin Ming and his team are entirely focusing on the task at hand. They're about to move the final tunnel section into position. Nothing on this scale has ever been attempted in China before. And Nature is on their side. The current turns exactly when they are expecting it to. The tunnel section arrives at the construction site on time.

LIN MING, Chief Tunnel Engineer

The first part's done. Now we're preparing to sink it. You can see the hooks keeping it in place. We have to remove some of them. We have to remove a lot of the equipment that we used during transportation. Until the eight big anchors are secured the risk is considerable. The sideways current will move it. If it enters the white area then we're in trouble.

Lin Ming's team is working on the installation of the last tunnel section

It's a race against time to install the section before the current pushed it out of position. Even if they didn't have to battle the current, placing the section in the right position underwater would still be a momentous task. Back in 2013 it took over 90 hours to install the first tunnel section.

LIN MING

We're only one team. We have to stay from beginning to end. When we enter the middle stage, some of them, like these operators, will be getting some sleep. They'll rest for three to five hours, but it's not proper rest. People can't turn themselves on or off just like a switch. They may fall asleep, get some rest, or they may not. It's a challenge. The long hours, the exhaustion, is definitely one of the challenges here. The first time, it took us 96 hours. A full 96 hours.

Tired technicians

Workers work overnight

Lin Ming hopes to complete the installation before daybreak. However, success will depend on more than just his team's ability to battle exhaustion. Subtle undercurrents could potentially endanger the entire process. Twice in the past three years, sudden changes in the situation in the water forced the team to suspend the installation.

While Lin and his colleagues face up to their own unique challenges, another team is simulating a worst-case scenario. The submerged tunnel lies 40 meters under the surface. Here, the slightest accident could spell disaster. In testing the tunnel's safety, they need to confirm that the key structure is capable of withstanding

Fire emergency test of the tunnel

Guardrail testing

temperatures up to 1,200 °C. They must also draw up emergency procedures for responding to an accident.

The guardrails on the bridge have gone through equally rigorous testing. A range of different vehicles were hurled at the barrier at speeds exceeding 100 kilometers per hour.

Back out at sea, Lin Ming's team is on the point of completing the project they've been working on for almost a decade. This is the last, and the most crucial part of the process. Section E30 is about to be lowered into the sea. There, it will slide in between the sections that have already been installed, completing the massive puzzle at the bottom of the sea.

LIN MING, Chief Tunnel Engineer

The sections have been connected. Now we have to make an inspection to check for foreign bodies and other issues. We need to check that the connection is right. Today's gone very smoothly. Our engineers have done an excellent job. It feels good, but it's not done yet. We can't say anything yet.

Once this is done we can connect them. We'll just give it one last pull. After that, the connection will be complete.

Over the last three years, Lin and his team have installed more than 30 tunnel sections, creating the longest submerged sea tunnel in the world. Their hope is that this mega project can serve as a blueprint for similar undertakings in the future – albeit with some modifications.

LIN MING

This bridge, this project, is unique. The methods we used here, if you use them in a different situation, won't necessarily work flawlessly. Engineers have to understand that.

In complex projects like this we're learning new methods. And we're passing on these methods – a way of thinking.

It's become more than a bridge to us. Some of us have worked here from the age of 30 to 40, some from 20 to 30. This project is part of our lives.

Successful installation of the last tunnel section

Lin Ming and his team cheering for the smooth installation of the last tunnel section

They have finally completed the installation of the final tunnel section. Now the inspection team will decide if they have been successful.

LUO XIONGBIN

LIAO JIANHUA

Underwater inspection of the tunnel section

LUO XIONGBIN, Diving Team Leader

Today, ten of our team will carry out an underwater inspection. We'll be checking the connection between Sections E30 and E31.

LIAO JIANHUA, Underwater Inspection Team Leader

The joints are sealed with a waterstop to keep water out. This prevents leaks. We'll check that the specifications are met and that the installation meets our standards. This is the first time in China that a tunnel has been laid in sections deep under water.

The inspection team will dive to 50 meters below the surface to assess the installation. Each team member will collect data from several key points along the tunnel section. The data is then transferred to the control ship, where engineers assess the findings with reference to the set standards.

I'm there.
Okay. Arriving at the section. Find your direction and head north. We see 9 mm, please confirm. Move the camera and confirm.

The team has a list of things to inspect. They must determine whether the new section has aligned properly with those installed previously, and whether the waterstops are functioning as they should.

The diver to inspect the installation of the tunnel section

LIAO JIANHUA

There are a lot of things that could go wrong. If the pressure's uneven or something's blocking the waterstop, the ability to keep water out is compromised.

The slightest irregularity can affect the performance of the entire tunnel. If a problem is found, it's up to Lin and his team to try and remedy the situation, which is likely to delay the completion of the entire project. However, the inspection team's findings are looking promising.

LIAO JIANHUA

Our inspection has found that it's looking pretty good. The connection and the pressure are even. Our evaluation is that the standard is high.

Today's success is the latest of many breakthroughs that have been achieved during the bridge's construction. It's expected that the new methods and technologies they've developed will be a help to Chinese engineers in the future. But how?

JING QIANG, Vice Director, Engineering Management Department, Hong Kong-Zhuhai-Macao Bridge Authority

My generation has grown up during a time of enormous economic growth in China. It may not be better than every other bridge in the world but I've realized it is different. One generation or one project may not be enough but if only we can appreciate this difference one day we'll build the best bridge in the world.

We're at the Guangdong Changda CB07 factory in Zhongshan. They produce aggregates. We're here to assess how stable the stone production is.

This is SMA? See how clean it is. Look at it. After touching it our hands are clean. There's no dust. This is the quality we can achieve. It may not be the best in the world but we've done the best we can as far as our capabilities and imagination allow us. With this attitude we can guarantee quality.

An aggregate production line

The Hong Kong-Zhuhai-Macao Bridge represents the pinnacle of decades of bridge-building achievement. More than that, it is an indication of where "Made in China" is headed in the future.

The adoption of robotic systems is one example of this. At the China Railway Shanhaiguan Bridge Group, the oldest bridge-building company in China, robotic systems have helped raise production to unprecedented levels.

Automatic welding system being used in the production of steel girders

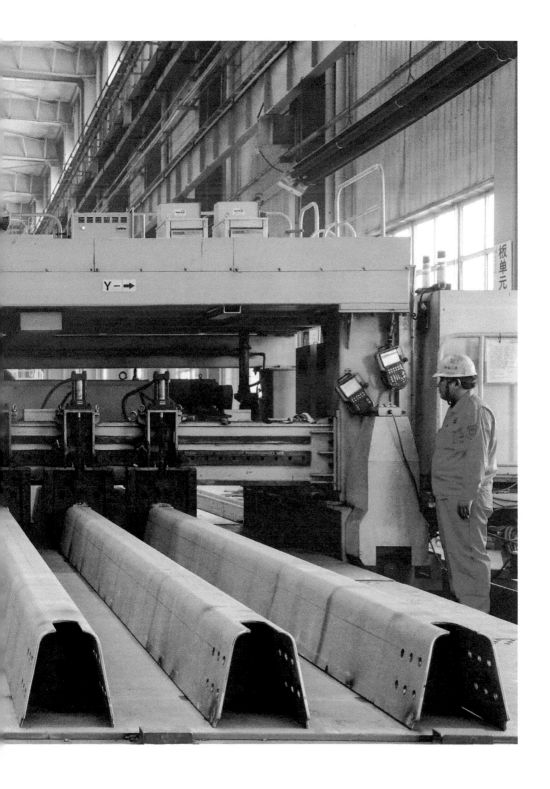

GUO CHANGJIANG

GUO CHANGJIANG, Representative, China Railway Shanhaiguan Bridge Group

I'm proud to say – and it's to my surprise – that although this part will normally have faults or dents, for the bridge I haven't found a single one. It's just one continuous weld. Car manufacturing uses a lot of robots. Bridge construction doesn't, but that changed with this bridge. The contractor wanted to introduce new technologies. How do you improve manufacturing? You begin with new processing methods.

Many people believe that the bridge has greater significance than its breakthroughs in construction methods and technologies.

SU QUANKE, Chief Engineer, Hong Kong-Zhuhai-Macao Bridge Authority

We've done more than just building

A section of the Hong Kong-Zhuhai-Macao Bridge in construction

a bridge and a tunnel. We've built a connection, a link. It's more than just a physical link. It connects our thoughts, our sentiments and the good things we've created together over the years. It has linked our technical standards. It has linked our regulations. It has linked our thinking.

It's been a month since Lin Ming's team installed the last tunnel section. Now they're back at the site to install the last joint. When the tunnel opens to traffic, Hong Kong on the east side of the Pearl River Delta will be connected with Zhuhai and Macao on the west. This will give the bridge its symbolic meaning.

JING QIANG

Initially, I was just building a bridge, but looking back now I realize that maybe what we built has set a lot of things in motion. For instance, when we were building the bridge we had to put forward all these ideas. To make use of them and achieve our goal a lot of things had to be updated, including the equipment, materials and technologies, as well as our ideas – everything, but people at my level may not see that.

A construction site of the bridge.

MENG FANCHAO, Chief Designer, Section DB01, Hong Kong-Zhuhai-Macao Bridge

From a technical point of view the bridge has a clear focus on aesthetics and bridge-building culture. Anyone who sees it will likely agree. This is more than a man-made structure. It's a cultural vehicle.

SU QUANKE, Chief Engineer, Hong Kong-Zhuhai-Macao Bridge Authority

So in building a bridge between these cities it's more than just a high quality, long lifespan, world-class project. It's something that affects local development and future projects in China, as well as international standards, systems and regulations. It's a fine example of how to build a bridge.

Some people admire the bridge's quality; others marvel at its projected long lifespan. Yet others prefer to focus on the time they spent with it.

ZHONG JIANRONG, Tunnel Builder

I was sent here by my company after I graduated. We're both from Huizhou in Guangdong. We've got a connection with Hong Kong, Macao and Zhuhai. Hong Kong and Macao were separated from the mainland for a while. Now that we have the bridge I think our lives will get better. We built this island and this bridge. It was very exciting. It was the most important time in our lives.

Bridges overcome barriers. Throughout history, they have brought people closer together. The Hong Kong-Zhuhai-Macao Bridge connects the Chinese mainland with Hong Kong and Macao. It also connects China with the rest of the world.

But this bridge does more than connecting regions. It connects China's past, its present and its future. After almost 70 years of development, China has grown from a fledgling that was only just learning to fly to a great bird spreading its wings and soaring into the sky. The concepts of "Chinese standards" and "Made in China" are increasingly making their impact felt on the world stage. As for the Hong Kong-Zhuhai-Macao Bridge, it is the latest, most impressive symbol of the Chinese Dream.

Zhong Jianrong, his wife and co-workers posing for pre-wedding photos

A worker's wedding
on the bridge

A section of the Hong Kong-Zhuhai-Macao Bridge

Movie

The Hong Kong-Zhuhai-Macao Bridge

Prelude

Planet Earth is largely covered by ocean,
The only thing bigger is the sky,
But the human mind is broader still.

In 2009, ambitious Chinese engineers started a project that would span the vast Lingding Sea in southern China.

Just 8 years later, they accomplished a miracle of human creation – the world's longest sea-crossing bridge.

Today, the spectacular Hong Kong-Zhuhai-Macao Bridge (HZMB) spans the Lingding Sea linking the three cities. Like a dragon in flight, it has reignited the confidence and dreams of the Chinese people.

A section of the Hong Kong-Zhuhai-Macao Bridge in construction

Attack of typhoon

News Report on August 23, 2017

"The 13th typhoon of this year, Hato, is going to hit the coast of Guangdong later today, bringing storms. The 7:00 a.m. update by the National Meteorological Center (NMC) has upgraded it to a severe typhoon."

"The West Artificial Island of the HZMB is still under intensive construction. It's a focal point of the typhoon relief work in Zhuhai."

"The municipal government has urgently evacuated 15,000 workers from the West Artificial Island."

"Local border guards, the police and public transport departments have mobilized 110 buses, 20 military trucks and over 300 civil vehicles to evacuate islanders in 20 batches since 19:00 on August 22."

"Typhoon Hato made landfall around 12:50 south of Zhuhai in Guangdong, bringing with it winds of up to force 14, making it a severe typhoon."

"The NMC has issued a red alert and raised the emergency natural disaster response to level II. Hong Kong and Macao have raised their alerts to the highest level. Bringing destructive gales and storm tides, Hato is as devastating as Typhoon Fred in 1991, and stronger than any other typhoon to land in Guangdong since August 1949."

"While the aftermath of Hato lingers, Paka arrives. The NMC has today renewed a yellow typhoon alert. Paka, the 14th typhoon of the year, is about to hit western Guangdong tomorrow."

"At around 9:00 a.m. today, the eye of Typhoon Paka made landfall southeast of Taishan City in Guangdong with maximum sustained wind speeds reaching force 12."

The Hong Kong-Zhuhai-Macao Bridge having withstood the test of typhoon

Voice-over

Sunshine returns after the typhoon. Just 50 days after its linking up, the HZMB stood strong in the Lingding Sea through the storms, to the amazement of the whole world.

As the world's longest sea-crossing bridge, the HZMB cost about 120 billion yuan to build. Spanning the Lingding Sea at the Pearl River estuary, the 55 kilometers structure starts at the Hong Kong boundary artificial island. After a 12 kilometers overpass, the roadway enters the world's longest subsea tunnel via the East Artificial Island, and runs for nearly 6.7 kilometers underwater. It then reaches the 22.9 kilometers main bridge at the West Artificial Island. Then, on the Zhuhai-Macao Boundary

The interior of the immersed tunnel of the Hong Kong-Zhuhai-Macao Bridge

Artificial Island, it splits and leads to Zhuhai and Macao respectively.

The megastructure has set many world records with its design and construction. In 2015, the British newspaper *The Guardian* named it one of the Seven Wonders of the Modern World.

The HZMB consists of bridges, islands and a tunnel. The 6.7 kilometers submerged tunnel is made of 33 connected tubes, making it one of the most difficult projects ever to have been built.

On May 2, 2013, the first tunnel tube was installed. In the four years that followed, Chinese engineers embedded the rest of the 33 segments one after another, carefully putting them into place underwater.

This is the last one, E30.

The 6.7 kilometers undersea tunnel will have its final piece in position.

But nothing miraculous is ever easy.

Caption

5:00 a.m., March 4, 2017, HZMB Construction Base Camp Dock

Voice-over

On March 4, 2017, the preparatory work begins. Sixty-year-old island-tunnel project chief engineer Lin Ming will lead his team to the installation area.

Born in 1957 in Xinghua, Jiangsu, Lin graduated with a degree in port construction. He started his career as a construction worker and finally became the general engineer of China Communications Construction. In December 2010, he was chosen as the general manager and chief engineer of the HZMB's island and tunnel projects.

The rubble-leveling ship Jinping 1

Caption

6:00 a.m., March 4, 2017, Tube E30 Installation Area

Voice-over

The Jinping 1, China's largest rubble-leveling ship, is totally home-developed and specially designed for the construction of the HZMB. It's one of the most crucial tools for building the world's longest immersed tunnel.

Actual sound

All systems aboard the rubble-levelling ship meet design specifications.

Has anything fallen off?

No.

Lin, the levelling of the last footing groove for E30 is ready to start, your order?

Go ahead!

Voice-over

Before laying tubes at a depth of over 40 meters, a footing groove needs to be dug at the seabed and covered with rubbles 2-3 meters thick.

The rubble-leveling ship is designed to tamp down and flatten the rubbles with an elevation error of less than 4 cm, creating a new composite foundation in the complex undersea geo-environment.

The world's most complicated construction technology today will ensure the precise docking of tubes and resist any water.

Interview

Lin Ming, Chief Engineer for the HZMB Island and Tunnel Projects

At that time, South Korea had a similar ship imported from Europe. I went to visit it accompanied by South Koreans. I wanted to get a closer view, but they said "no." So we turned to Shanghai Zhenhua Heavy Industry (ZPMC) for help. This ship was then built to complete the

Construction of an artificial island for the Hong Kong-Zhuhai-Macao Bridge

project.

Voice-over

Such a mammoth undersea project is unprecedented.

Chinese engineers demarcated a battlefield covering over 1,000 square kilometers at sea. Nearby, they also set up a base camp and built plants to produce various bridge parts.

They felt their way forward, dealing with challenges as they arose. Many world-class problems were solved, many world records were broken and over 400 patents were acquired.

The completed artificial island

Interview

Lin Ming

We have the wisdom to find solutions to every problem, drawing on global and international resources.

The achievements of Chinese engineers make us feel proud!

Caption

Niutou Island - Tunnel Tube Production Base

Voice-over

Everything is ready for the coming final battle.

The Lingding Sea has some of the world's busiest seaports and airports. Every day, more than 4,000 ships and over 1,800 planes come and go. Near the main waterway sit the airports of Hong Kong, Macao, Zhuhai and Shenzhen. Planes will fly past the area less than 1 minute after takeoff, which means no structure may be higher than 120 meters.

The only way to build a cross-sea bridge over such a busy channel is to combine bridges with islands and tunnels.

But such islands didn't exist.

A still of the 1955 documentary *"Move Mountains, Fill the Sea"*

In 2009, China adopted the most imaginative plan in its bridge construction history. Up to 120 giant steel cylinders were to be erected on the seabed, and filled with soil to quickly create an artificial island.

Each cylinder is 22.5 meters in diameter and 40 to 50 meters high, equivalent to the height of a 20-storey building.

Compared with traditional methods, the new technique shortened the construction period and reduced the volume of silt dredging by nearly 10 million cubic meters.

The two artificial islands just look like two anchored aircraft carriers. Between them, there is a 6.7 kilometers immersed tunnel.

But 60 years ago, such a miraculous project was almost impossible to imagine.

To link the mainland and Xiamen Island in 1954, over 3,000 poorly equipped workers built a 5 kilometers long seawall through land reclamation. A 1955 documentary *"Move Mountains, Fill the Sea"* recorded that process.

Caption

5:00 a.m., March 6, 2017, Niutou Island

A section of the Hong Kong-Zhuhai-Macao Bridge stretching across the Lingding Sea

Interview

Lin Ming

After three years, this will be the last time. When we were taking photos yesterday, many of the captains shed tears. They showed me one text message "Is our work really done?" So many difficulties and problems were overcome during construction.

It hasn't been easy to keep going. It's hard to say goodbye.

It's the end of an era.

Caption

6:00 a.m.

Voice-over

The last tube is about to leave the dock.

But heavy fog over the Lingding Sea worries Lin.

Discussions over a bridge across the Lingding Sea began in 1983. But the significantly different legal systems and construction standards of the three cities meant it was more than a technical challenge for Chinese engineers.

Interview

Meng Fanchao, Chief Designer of HZMB DB01 Bridge Section

The HZMB links the places in one country but under two systems, making it unique in the world.

We have built cross-border projects before. But this one connecting three cities in one country, but with two systems, is the first of its kind worldwide.

As the HZMB combines bridges, islands and an immersed tunnel, it makes us think about the Chinese idiom – A perfect pairing of pearls and jade.

Interview

Su Quanke, Chief Engineer, Hong Kong-Zhuhai-Macao Bridge Authority

What we've built is a link.

It begins with the Zhuhai Connecting Road, consisting of 4 tunnels, 4 artificial islands and over 40 kilometers of bridges. The cities, islands, tunnels and bridges, if put together, just look like pearls connected by a silver thread.

Voice-over

A silver thread has connected the pearls that dot the Lingding Sea. To Chinese people, this area is familiar yet strange. Over 700 years ago here, Wen Tianxiang wrote his famous poem: All men are mortal, but my loyalty will illuminate the annals of history forever. Over the past centuries, Eastern and Western civilizations have embraced each other

Qiantang River Bridge, which was once blown up in the War of Resistance against Japanese Aggression

Completion of Wuhan Yangtze River Bridge (1957)

here. Today, Chinese engineers are describing the close integration of the three cities along the Linding Sea as the perfect pairing of pearls and jade.

Voice-over

The history of China's modern bridge construction started in a war 80 years ago.

In the 1930s, 39-year-old Mao Yisheng was given the job of building a bridge over the Qiantang River, thought by foreigners to be unbridgeable.

But after 37 months of hard work, Chinese engineers completed the 1,453-meter Qiantang River Bridge.

However, the breakout of the Battle of Shanghai forced Mao into a sad decision to blow it up.

Just 89 days after it came into use, China's first modern road-rail bridge had to be destroyed in the face of Japanese aggression.

After its founding in 1949, the People's Republic of China started to bridge mountains and rivers.

In 1957, the Wuhan Yangtze River Bridge opened. As the first bridge over the river, it's called the "First Bridge of the Yangtze." In 1968, another bridge was completed. The Nanjing Yangtze River Bridge was the first to be designed and built independently by China over the Yangze.

The bridges that cross rivers and connect the arteries of southern and northern China fulfilled a dream that had lasted thousands of years across the Yangtze River.

While swimming in the Wuhan section of the Yangtze River, Chairman Mao Zedong hailed the Wuhan Yangtze River Bridge, "spanning the north and south, turning a deep chasm into a busy thoroughfare."

Overcoming mountains and rivers, Chinese bridges have been not only carried the hopes of the nation, but also attracted the attention of the country's leaders. In 1993, 89-year-old Deng Xiaoping came to the Yangpu Bridge in Shanghai. Enthused by the country's great achievements since 1978, the elder statesman uncharacteristically turned to poetry: Wonderful to see the road we have walked, outperform all books we have read.

Time never stands still. After rapid development of engineering technology since 1978, China has become the world's top bridge builder.

Throughout the country, the over 1 million bridges, linking urban and rural areas, have helped turn the whole of China into a mammoth fast developing economy.

The bridge frenzy in China is more than just a joke among netizens.

Today, whether it's over the mountains, by the sea or in the sky, the Chinese people are fulfilling their dreams.

Caption

6:10 a.m., Niutou Island

Steel box girders

Voice-over

Despite 32 successful installations, the last tube brought Lin greater pressure.

Steel box girders

Actual sound

The installation of E29 has been completed, right? Yes, so after that, it's turn for E30.

The installation of E29 was allowed to involve some errors that we can fix during the installation of E30. But now, there is no room for error. E29 is in place and E30 must dock with it perfectly. Of all the tubes, the last one is subject to the most constraints. The pressure on us is great. Just now, I talked about calmness. But it's hard. Nobody can keep calm.

I beg every one of you to do me a favor and try your best to do everything well. Let's make it easy for everyone, OK? Thank you very much!

Huang, keep a close eye on things.

Interview

Lin Ming

There is quite a lot of pressure on me. Man proposes, but God disposes. As an old Chinese saying goes "Neither effort nor luck is dispensable." Lots of things are beyond your capability.

Shipment of steel box girders

Voice-over

The HZMB spans the Pearl River estuary. Limits to flow retardation and the need to be able to withstand a magnitude-8 earthquake and force-16 typhoon pose new challenges to its design.

Traditional concrete frame structures are not enough to meet the requirements for a long span, which also needs to be lightweight. Engineers decide to use steel box girders.

Interview

Jing Qiang

To make each steel box section, a series of steel plate units were built in sequence until the box structure took shape. The plates were brought here and then welded together into small girder sections that were then

Hydraulic pressure vehicles for moving steel box girders

assembled to form larger sections.

Voice-over

The main bridge of the HZMB consists of 2,156 girders. The total weld length is about 1.2 million meters.

That is the distance between Beijing and Shanghai.

Every centimeter of welding decides the lifespan of the bridge.

Interview

Jing Qiang

The HZMB project adopted a "life-cycle monitoring system" for bridge part production, from material sourcing right up until the part took shape.

Mounting the steel box girder

Voice-over

At the Zhongshan Production Base, the first steel box girder of the HZMB is to be shipped to the construction site over 30 kilometers away.

It's 132.6 meters long, 33.1 meters wide and weighs 2,815 tons.

The 896 wheels of the 8 hydraulic platform trailers need to keep in step with each other. But this whole process is overseen by just one person.

The 220-meter move of 2,815 tons created another world record.

The girder carried by a barge arrives at the installation site after a 24-hour sea trip. Two maritime Hercules are waiting for it. They are nicknamed "the arms of the nation."

Back in the 1950s and 1960s, China's maritime cranes were mainly used at ports and docks. Even being able to lift little more than 100 tons seemed exciting at the time.

File

Peking Opera *The Harbor*
How spectacular the dock looks
Machines line up on the river bank
What an awesome crane it is
Tons of steel is lifted so easily
Hahaha...

Voice-over

Through the constant development of China's manufacturing sector, crane boats less than 10,000 tons have become commonplace.

Meanwhile, jumbo crane vessels able to lift over 12,000 tons are already standing by.

Caption

7:00 a.m., Niutou Island

Voice-over

A dense fog over the Lingding Sea is yet to disperse, but preparations

The installation team of tunnel sections is ready for work

The installation team of tunnel sections conducting a ceremony, hoping that the work will be accomplished successfully

are already getting underway.

Actual sound

Maritime Patrol Ship

0188, leave the area please.

The HZMB tunnel construction work is underway here. Leave now, please.

Mobilization Conference

Our success or failure will capture attention from people nationwide and worldwide.

I believe we will complete the task successfully and meet the expectations of the governments and people in the mainland, Hong Kong and Macao.

7:30 a.m., Niutou Island

Interview

Lin Ming

Currently at sea, we have about 400 employees and nearly 40 vessels. This is our team.

This is the tube. Our plan is as follows: four ships are arranged here with another four over there. Usually we have eight tugboats. During the trip, we sail along a waterway about 200 meters wide. Out this way, the water is not deep enough. This place was once a quarry. We chose it and used its natural conditions to create the best undocking environment at the least cost.

Voice-over

Niutou Island in the Lingding Sea used to be uninhabited. Engineers turned it into the world's largest steel box girder plant to produce 33 of the world's longest submerged tunnel tubes for the HZMB.

A distant view of the precast plant of tunnel sections in Niutou Island

Most of the tubes are 180 meters long and 38 meters wide, 16 times the area of a basketball court. Each of them weighs nearly 80,000 tons, equal to the displacement of a large aircraft carrier.

The 33 tubes are made from 330,000 tons of steel bars and over 2 million tons of concrete, enough to build eight 828-meter high Burj Khalifa Towers.

A close shot of the precast plant of tunnel sections

Interview

Hans De Wit, Dutch Engineer

These are by far the biggest immersed tunnel elements that have ever been used. I've been in China since 2008, when they started the project. They started it from scratch, developing the technologies and introducing innovations that were thoroughly tested and studied, and made sure that they could meet the very stringent requirements...

Voice-over

China's increasing overall strength has led to a series of breakthroughs in bridge design, bridge material production and bridge construction. Just half a century later, the country has become a competent world class bridge builder.

The HZMB was designed with a lifespan of 120 years, to international standards. This further cements China's role as a bridge construction powerhouse.

ZHANG JINWEN, Project Director, Hong Kong-Zhuhai-Macao Bridge Authority

The material used in the bridge deck pavement

Interview

Zhang Jinwen, Project Director, Hong Kong-Zhuhai-Macao Bridge Authority

We've used the finest materials to surface the bridge. We have adopted processing methods prevailing in the precision chemical and food industries. The precasting of tunnel tubes and pier bases, the production and processing of steel box girders, the surfacing work, as well as the gravel processing, were completed to industrial standards. We want transportation construction to share the high standards seen in manufacturing sector.

The welding robot at China Railway Shanhaiguan Bridge Group

The workshop with welding robots at China Railway Shanhaiguan Bridge Group

Voice-over

China Railway Shanhaiguan Bridge Group is the birthplace of China's steel bridges.

To meet the technological standards of the HZMB, a robotic welding system was developed. The respected factory ended up with the world's largest and most precise automatic steel box girder production line.

Two Chinese white dolphins playing with each other

Interview

Guo Changjiang, Chairman, China Railway Shanhaiguan Bridge Group

I'm proud. The fact that none of common weld defects such as arc strike cracking and crater crack were found in the HZMB was beyond my expectations. The auto industry has widely used robots, but the steel bridge building sector didn't adopt it until the HZMB constructor resolved to lead the technological development in the industry. That development should start with the upgrading of processing methods.

Voice-over

Besides a series of breakthroughs, the bridge also set another example.

The winding Hong Kong-Zhuhai-Macao Bridge

The HZMB construction area touches on the Chinese White Dolphin Natural Reserve. The endangered animal was the official mascot of the 1997 handover ceremonies in Hong Kong.

Before the project broke ground, engineers had promised to complete the bridge while also preserving the home of dolphins.

Monitoring results show that when the project was complete, about 1,890 dolphins were still living in waters around the bridge.

On July 20, 2017, the construction site once again embraces sunshine after rain. The first dolphin that had been rescued here was released into the sea in the presence of construction workers and nature reserve staff.

When it comes to relations between human and nature, Chinese philosophy emphasizes respect for nature and opposes anything that goes against it.

Interview

Su Quanke

From here we can see that the bridge bends. It runs from Zhuhai and Macao to Hong Kong – that's a given. But why can't it be straight? It'd be shorter, right? It's because of the shipping lanes, which need to follow the sea currents. Unlike a river, sea currents are changeable. The bridge needs to bend to create a straight angle with the currents. That's why we get this bend. Still, it's quite attractive.

Voice-over

The ancient Chinese were some of the earliest and most prolific bridge-builders in the world. This is hardly surprising, since the country's territory is marked by thousands of crisscrossing rivers. Even in the most remote village, evidence can be found of ancient bridges, built using local materials and know-how.

Interview

Su Quanke

Bridges in China, on top of the basic engineering, incorporate a lot of art and are imbued with meaning. In every bridge they build the Chinese instill cultural connotations.

Caption

10:00 a.m., Waters off Niutou Island

Actual sound

(Inside a Cabin)
Tugboat 4 is joining the formation. Everything is going well. Over.
This is what we want, water retardation coefficient.

Lin Ming and his team

Voice-over

This is not only China's first immersed tunnel project in the open sea, but also the world's most difficult construction project, with no examples to follow.

At first, Chinese builders were expecting help from a foreign specialist firm. But they asked 1.5 billion yuan in consultancy fees and insisted that China could do nothing without foreign assistance.

Interview

Lin Ming

Without an instructor the pressure was immense. It was very tough, but because we had no one to help us we were able to develop our own methods.

Voice-over

Finally, they overcame many world-class problems, and miraculously prevented any water seeping into the open-sea sections of the submerged tunnel.

Interview

Lin Ming

When we did this for the first time, I felt I was just like a rookie driver on the first road run. But now, I'm already a veteran.

Voice-over

The mega century project over the Lingding Sea is hailed as the "Mount Qomolangma of Bridges." How will it affect the people living in the Pearl River Delta? We can find clues in New York Bay.

This is the annual cross-city bike ride in New York.

Actual sound

New York Citizens

Yes I am living here for six years already, and the bridges are a very important part of New York City as a whole.

I mean you stand down below and you look up at the sky and see them against the horizon, and they're beautiful.

To know New York, you have to know its bridges first.

Voice-over

New York, the largest port city in the US, is also the global trade and financial center.

It is divided into several parts by rivers. The city only covers 1,200 square kilometers, including water area. That about the same as the combined area of Hong Kong and Macao.

But it has around 2,000 bridges of different sizes, ensuring 8.5 million New Yorkers fully enjoy the prosperity of an integrated New York Bay.

The city clusters on the two sides of the Pearl River Delta cover less than 1% of China's territory, but create 13% of its GDP.

Today, the bay area economy is part of the national strategy. The Guangdong-Hong Kong-Macao Greater Bay Area will be built into a world-class bay and city cluster.

The prosperous Pearl River Delta

Interview

Wei Dongqing, Executive Director, Hong Kong-Zhuhai-Macao Bridge Authority

The Guangdong-Hong Kong-Macao Greater Bay Area accommodates over 60 million people and has the most advanced market economy in China. It's the first place in the country to go global and also the birthplace of modern Chinese ideology.

Voice-over

But the vast Lingding Sea has hindered contact between the east and west sides of the Pearl River Delta, hampering the further economic development in the region.

People on both sides shared a common dream.

Today, the milestone HZMB over the Lingding Sea is set to help fulfill this dream.

Interview

Chris Chan, Chairman of the Macao Air Freight Forwarding (Logistics) Association (MAFFA)

Currently, sea transport is the only way for logistics services between Hong Kong and Macao, and that takes a whole day. But with the opening of the HZMB, that's down to just 30 minutes.

Interview

Lawmaker Si Ka Lon, Legislative Assembly of Macao
For Macao, the bridge will absolutely add to its competiveness.

Caption

2:00 p.m., Lingding Sea

Lin Ming is commanding the towage of tunnel sections

Towage of tunnel sections

The tugboat is towing the tunnel sections

Actual sound

Got it.

Is my ship in the middle?

You've drifted to the right a little. It's OK. That's fine.

Tugboat 1, tell him. 15 degrees or 10 degrees. Tell him.

You've deflected 30 degrees from the median.

OK. I'll turn left 30 degrees.

Tugboat 1, stop.

Your captain is excellent. Boat 11 did well. Boat 1 was unsteady. So, boat 11 might want to take the place of boat 1.

It's much better than I expected. I saw everything I wanted to see. Once it was just records in books. But now, we can see all this for ourselves. I remember all the speeds. I will write a report soon.

Interview

Lin Ming

Nobody else would create a full scale model for an experiment at sea. But we did it today. It's good. That will provide vital data for future domestic projects. We can also share it with the outside world.

Caption

Tunnel Fire Prevention Experiment Base, Zhangzhou, Fujian

Simulation test of fire emergency in the tunnel of the Hong Kong-Zhuhai-Macao Bridge

Actual sound

All teams in position!
Wind velocity team is ready!
Data collection team is ready!
Fire team is ready!
Wind team, start data collection!
3, 2, 1, light it up now!

Jiang Shuping, Chief Expert of Chongqing Communications Technology Research & Design Institute Co., Ltd.

Performance test of the Hong Kong-Zhuhai-Macao Bridge's guardrails against crash

Performance test of the Hong Kong-Zhuhai-Macao Bridge's guardrails against crash

Voice-over

What if a fire were to break out in an undersea tunnel?

Response plans for such emergencies worldwide lacked scientific study.

After two years of hard work, Chinese engineers have developed Chinese standards for the rescue and relief of undersea tunnel disasters, gaining international recognition.

Interview

Chai Shuping, Chongqing Communications Technology Research & Design Institute Company Limited

A lot of data were gathered for the first time. There were many scientific findings and many results that have practical application for construction projects.

Voice-over

The bridge's safety always comes first. To that end, engineers created a set of simulation devices to check whether the guardrails can withstand the impact of a vehicle travelling at over 100 km/h.

Today, is the trend of bridge technology still led by Western countries? Actually, no.

Interview

Meng Fanchao

Prior to the 1970s, where was the global center of bridge building? In Europe and America. From the 1970s to the early 21st century, where was this center then? In Japan. The Japanese, after their economy took off, built some of the world's greatest cross-sea bridges and tunnels. Since the early 21st century, you could say this center is in China.

Mobilization for safe operation by installation workers of tunnel sections

The workers are satisfying their hunger with simple food after working for a long time

Voice-over

After decades of rapid growth, China has transformed itself from a follower to a frontrunner in bridge technology development. Every year, it sets new world records in bridge construction. It also holds more than half of the world's top 10 records for every bridge category.

Caption

10:30 p.m., March 6, Installation Site

Actual sound

On deck

1, 2, 3, safety first!

Bread and ham sausage are his "working meal"

Voice-over

Hauled by 60,000 horsepower, the 80,000-ton tube is drifted 12 kilometers in 15 hours and is now held steady at the dive site.

Interview

Lin Ming

Before the dive, we need to install and calibrate many devices for the docking procedure. We only have one team that needs to do everything from start to finish. Fatigue during the nonstop work is a big challenge for us in this phase.

People in Linxian County were working hard to dig the Red Flag Canal

The installation of the 1st tube took 96 hours. 96 hours, the first time. That's the longest period without sleep in my life, five days and four nights.

Voice-over

China's construction history is one of overcoming difficulties and challenges.

To fight drought in the 1960s, people in Linxian County, Henan Province spent 10 years digging over 70 kilometers Red Flag Canal along the face of sheer cliffs through the Taihang Mountains entirely by hand. That put an end to the long-term water scarcity there.

The Guoliang Cave in the Taihang Mountains

Wang Chaoying, a keen photographer

Also deep in the Taihang Mountains, over 300 residents in Guoliang Village used to live on cliffs. To ease the access to outside world, the villagers spent six years in the 1970s carving out the 1,300m Guoliang Tunnel through the mountains, mostly with only hammers and chisels.

In China's history, heroes brave enough to fight natural adversities have never been in short supply.

Voice-over

Engineer Wang Chaoying is a keen photographer.

Interview

Wang Chaoying, Worker Photographer

The steel box girder production for the HZMB involved a whole family. Three generations of Feng's family, including Mr. and Mrs. Feng, contributed to the project. They are happy. They built the bridge. They feel proud. They know what this responsibility means.

Another set of photos are named Yanzi and her husband. The wife at first was her husband's apprentice but later became his teacher. The couple

Three generations of Feng's family

Yanzi and her husband

Bright smile of participants in the construction of the Hong Kong-Zhuhai-Macao Bridge

The participants in the construction of the Hong Kong-Zhuhai-Macao Bridge are proud of their work

completed the welding work on an entire girder. Her work was exempt from crack detection and had a pass rate of 100 percent.

Of the people who have seen this photo, none guessed correct their ages, including me. They were born in 1979 and always smiled like that. Their smiles are sincere which nobody can simulate.

All bridge builders feel sincerely proud, including me. It's not something you can fake. Unlike smiles of performers during a show that look fake, theirs are pure. A sense of achievement makes them feel proud of working for the HZMB. The words Hong Kong, Zhuhai and Macao really mean something to us.

Voice-over

For some others, they prefer to recall the time they spent with the bridge.

Interview

Zhong Jianrong, Worker for HZMB Island and Tunnel Project

This is the first project in my career. Working for such a big project leaves me with a beautiful memory. It's so cool.

With his colleagues, Zhong Jianrong and his wife are taking pre-wedding photos on the bridge

Hong Kong and Macao were once separated from the mainland for quite some time. I believe the bridge will help improve our communications.

Voice-over

On the tallest pylons of the HZMB, there are steel "Chinese knots," which represent an eternal wish of the Chinese people for friendship.

Interview

We built this island and this bridge.
It was very exciting. It was the most important time in our lives.
He spent over five years here and I stayed for over two years.
In our minds, each of us has two lovers: our wives and this project.

Caption

3:00 a.m., March 7, 2017, Dive Site

Tube E15

Actual sound

Lin Ming

Is everyone in position?
Yes, all in position.
Pals, we'll sink the 33rd tube, be careful!

Voice-over

Forty meters below the sea surface, a giant dragon is waiting quietly.

Actual sound

Dive starts in 10 minutes. Be ready!

Voice-over

A colossus of 80,000 tons is about to sink into the seabed.

Caption

3:40 a.m.

Actual sound

Command Center
Be careful!
Notice the ship's sea gauge.
At the depth of 3 meters.
Copy that.
8 centimeters already.
Assess again when it's done.
We will make it in one go.
At the depth of 4 meters.
4 meters down already.

Voice-over

This is the world's most difficult undersea tunnel project. An accident could happen anytime no matter how careful you are. During the installation of tube E15 two years ago, Lin's team failed twice as the footing groove silted up suddenly.

Caption

February 24, 2015 (Day 6 after Spring Festival)

Voice-over

On February 24, 2015, three months after the first failure, tube E15 sets out again after intensive preparation.

Actual sound

The 72 to 75-meter section between here and the eastern end has an excessive amount of silt.

The workers are upset with the failure of the second installation of tube E15

Voice-over

But luck was once again against them. The footing groove had been largely silted up again. A full box of silt brought back by divers surprised everyone.

Actual sound

Silt is everywhere.

In some places, we even can't reach its bottom when stretching our arms.

Voice-over

Groove silting is sand and mud deposition in the footing groove before tube installation. This time, the sediment depth is up to 60 cm. The tube will be hard to install smoothly.

Actual sound

Lin Ming

We may have to withdraw.

Our challenge is too powerful. The ocean, nature and the principles have been in existence for millions of years. How much can we learn

Lin Ming is having a rest

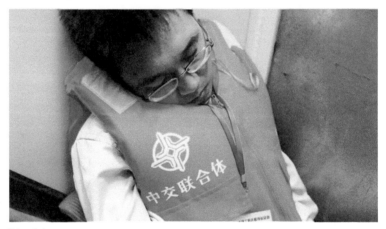

Exhausted

about them in such a short period? I think we have done well enough.

Voice-over

Lin's team has to tow back the 80,000-ton tube again.

The tired worker

Caption

March 24, 2015

Voice-over

A month later, E15 sets sail for the third time.

Actual sound

All set for the third-time towing and installation of tube E15. Your instruction?

Go ahead!

Voice-over

After over 50 hours of hard work, good news surfaces from 40 meters beneath the surface, but there is no applause.

Nobody wants to speak.

On the way back, engineers under stress and fatigue relax as best they can.

Everyone knows the final victory is still far away.

Caption

4:30 a.m. March 7, 2017

Actual sound

At the depth of 5 meters now.
Copy that.
Roger that.

Voice-over

Lin always suggests that 60% of your attention be paid to looking for potential risks.

Every time before a tube installation, risk prevention and control work includes over 230 procedures.

Actual sound

Test all systems once.

Voice-over

The 80,000-ton giant will be docked over 40 meters beneath the sea surface and with an error of less than 3 cm. Everyone knows how difficult it is. Engineers call it the "deep sea kiss."

Actual sound

Dive completed.
Are divers already in place?
Yes, they are checking now.

Voice-over

Divers need to reach the installation position, collect data at certain places and send them to the control room.

Actual sound

Subsea Inspection Ship
Divers reach the docking position.
Divers, judge direction, go northward.
Go northward, along the waterproof belt, check the belt.
The reading is 9 mm, please confirm, remove the camera, confirm with your eye.

The last tunnel section has been installed. The workers are listening to the report

Deviate 5mm northward?

Deviate 5mm northward, please confirm.

Voice-over

The quality supervision team is tasked with a wide-ranging assessment, including checking whether the new tube was installed in line with design specifications and whether the waterproof seal works well.

Actual sound

Tube Installation Ship

The towing, mooring, diving, docking and hydraulic crimping procedures have been completed. The monitoring system shows the tube installation accuracy meets design specifications. The installation of all 33 tunnel tubes has been accomplished. That's it. What's your instruction?

It's Fine!

Voice-over

At 9:00 a.m. on March 7, after nearly 26 hours of effort, the last tunnel tube E30 of the HZMB was docked successfully. Chinese engineers thus accomplished a miracle of human endeavor.

The 6.7 kilometers immersed tunnel realizes a historic crossing under the sea.

Interview

Lin Ming

It's become more than a bridge to us. Some of us have worked here from the age of 30 to 40, some from 20 to 30. This project is part of our lives.

Actual sound

"Well done! Thank you, everyone!"

Voice-over

The Lingding Sea was best known through the poem "A Helpless Sign in the Lingding Sea."

Today, the world's longest sea bridge has straddled it. A sigh deep in history has turned into a rainbow between the sea and the sky. Like a dragon starting to take off, it has ignited the confidence and dream of the Chinese people.

Presenting the Hong Kong-Zhuhai-Macao Bridge on TV and in the Movie Theater

The bridge tower in the shape of Chinese knot on the
Hong Kong-Zhuhai-Macao Bridge

Success
and
Impact

On June 30 and July 1, 2017, when the main body of the Hong Kong-Zhuhai-Macao Bridge (the Bridge) was nearly completed as a tribute to the 20th anniversary of resumption of China's exercise of sovereignty over Hong Kong, the TV documentary *The Hong Kong-Zhuhai-Macao Bridge* was broadcast successively on China Central Television (CCTV) and China Global Television Network (CGTN). In the meantime, it was distributed and disseminated on multimedia platforms throughout China, attracting a total of about 60 million non-repeat viewers. By July 2, the documentary had been watched by nearly 450 million viewers through terminals of CCTV.com, and had been hit and/or watched online more than 37.54 million times. Within one week, social media platform views overseas totaled close to 1.22 million. This meant a new round of "chat-room fever" and a new round of applause for the Bridge caused by the broadcasting of the documentary.

"It's a documentary that promotes the accomplishments of the Chinese people, builds up confidence in the Chinese road, and stimulates positive energy in society," one netizen commented.

Multiple newspapers, such as *Guangming Daily*, *Wen Yi Bao*, *Southern Metropolis Daily* and *Zhujiang Evening News*, gave in-depth press coverage of the Bridge and the TV documentary. *Wen Yi Bao* called the documentary "a homage to the project of the century" that "helps boost China's national strategy." The news bureau of the CPC Central Committee's Publicity Department stated in its newsletter that the documentary ignited the audience's patriotism and served as a tribute to the 20th anniversary of Hong Kong's return to China.

In January 2018, *The Hong Kong-Zhuhai-Macao Bridge* was elected one of the Top Ten TV Documentaries for 2017 out of more than 700 contenders. It won the honorary title at an award ceremony held in Zhengding, Hebei Province for "documenting a miracle of the current century."

The 55 kilometers Hong Kong-Zhuhai-Macao Bridge, the world's longest cross-sea bridge, connects the Hong Kong Special Administrative Region in the east and the Macao Special Administrative Region and the Chinese mainland city of Zhuhai in the west. The main body of the bridge consists of 22.9 kilometers of bridges, 6.7 kilometers of submerged tube tunnels and two artificial islands. The design life of the Bridge is 120 years. The Bridge symbolizes the close link between three regions under the "One Country, Two Systems" framework. It's also a new brand name highlighting China's connection to the world.

The TV documentary was co-produced by the Science and Education Channel of CCTV, the Hong Kong-Zhuhai-Macao Bridge Authority, Discovery Channel, Guangdong Radio and Television (GRT) and Zhuhai Radio and Television (ZHRT). It is also the first project of in-depth cooperation between CCTV and Discovery. Discovery is a widely distributed subscription channel of world renown, with an accumulative audience of three billion in over 220 countries and regions. Broadcasting of *The Bridge* on CCTV and Discovery can be seen as having built a bridge of communication between China and the world.

By telling China's story from an international perspective, the documentary expects to help foreigners "understand, comprehend and appreciate China better," said Yan Dong, director of the TV project.

Origin

Yan has a wealth of experience making full-length TV documentaries in the history and culture category. His main works include *Lu Xun School of the Arts*, *National Museum of China 100 Years*, *Confucius*, *Memories of Nanjing 1937*, *Main Battlefield in the East* and *The Long March*. *The Bridge*, however, is his first TV documentary in the engineering category involving an ongoing major national project. He knew he had to do a lot of homework in advance. At the invitation of his former schoolmate Guo Lin, head of ZHRT, Yan sequestered himself on a small island in Zhuhai and went over all videos about the Bridge produced over the years by ZHRT before spending an entire day visiting and observing the Bridge and interviewing engineers and builders. Though yet unfinished, Yan found the Bridge "magnificent and awe-inspiring," especially when viewed from the sea, and decided to take on the documentary project against many odds.

Yan Dong (right) at the premiere of the documentary *The Hong Kong-Zhuhai-Macao Bridge*

At a factory workshop in Zhongshan, Yan marveled at the minuteness of the sand particles used. "The smallest sand particles are even finer than those applied to facial exfoliating scrubs... Can you imagine a humongous bridge being pieced together by things that small? Such pursuit of detail is the very essence of art!" he exclaimed.

Yan demanded that all members of his team, whether directors, cameramen, or post-production people, visit the construction site and see the bridge with their own eyes so that they may develop a bonding with it. "Bonding and passion for the job is what separates creativeness from mundaneness and routine," he said.

Bai Li, Discovery's Distribution President in China, attributed the success of the co-production to the appeal of the Bridge. "It's the splendor of the bridge that drew us together," she said.

Vikram Channa, Vice President of Programming of Discovery Networks Asia-Pacific (DNAP), a division of Discovery, Inc., shared that thought. "Civil engineering wonders like the Hong Kong-Zhuhai-Macao Bridge always have a shocking effect!" he said.

Co-Director Kenny PNG, who is Chinese Singaporean, said that he initially had no interest in the project when Discovery solicited him for service. "I got bored directing engineering-themed documentaries," he said, "but Vikram kept saying I would change my mind after a field visit to the Bridge." Kenny did visit it and had a cozy ride on it. "Even the ups and downs feel nice and steady," he said of the experience.

Director Li Kai from ZHRT joined the team and filmed the Bridge from beginning to end. He loved the project and marveled how the builders brought the Bridge to pass across Lingding Sea within just nine years.

Story Ideas

Yan Dong saw the documentary as a story told to an international audience. In recent years, he has been working hard producing TV documentaries geared to a global audience. His earlier works, such as *Memories of Nanjing* 1937, *Main Battlefield in the East*, *The War That Changed the World*, *Confucius* and *The Long March*, are all well-told "China stories." Through active probing and successful practice, Yan has gained deep and unique insight on the making of "mainstream theme" documentaries.

"On September 28, 2015, President Xi Jinping delivered a speech entitled *Working Together to Forge a New Partnership of Win-win Cooperation and Create a Community of Shared Future for Mankind* at the 70th Session of the United Nations General Assembly. It marked the first time he presented and explained in detail 'a community of shared future for mankind,' a concept that sheds a lot of light on my TV projects. In his Report to the 19th CPC National Congress, Xi reiterated the importance of promoting the building of a community of shared future for mankind and the construction of a new type of international relations that features mutual respect, fairness and justice and win-win cooperation," Yan said.

On January 6, 2018, Yan Dong was asked to make a keynote speech at the 12th Awarding Ceremony for Chinese Documentaries in Zhengding, Hebei Province. In that speech entitled *From China's Mainstream Theme to the World's Mainstream Theme*, he said: "Mainstream-theme documentaries are no longer about major historical events and revolutionary subjects in the traditional sense. Instead, they should be centered on the idea of a community of shared future for mankind. This should be the mainstream theme not just for China, but also for the world."

Yan Dong's professional suavity made him realize from the start that the Hong Kong-Zhuhai-Macao Bridge was going to be a good subject showcasing the idea of "a community of shared future for mankind." He thinks that the Bridge has an international nature of its own because it's an ongoing story told in the global language of civil engineering. "Construction of the Bridge involved experts from multiple countries. It connects three regions, including some of the world's most dynamic economic zones. The increased integration of the three regions will lead to the forming of a mega metropolitan bay area covering Guangdong Province, Hong Kong SAR and Macao SAR. It will become the center of the world's attention!" Yan said.

Vikram Channa was passionate and confident about the co-production of the project. "The Hong Kong-Zhuhai-Macao Bridge is the world's longest cross-sea bridge. Since satisfying people's curiosity has always been Discovery's mission, we are curious and eager to uncover how China's engineers and workers completed this great project," Channa said.

Sunset at the Hong Kong-Zhuhai-Macao Bridge

While the crew team had no more than nine months to complete the filming project, Yan spent about four months doing research, team build-up and other preparatory work. Limited time meant the team had to get the communication channels straight from the start. The team seized every opportunity to communicate, whether by phone, through video conferences or face-to-face discussions, on a broad scope of issues. Any consensus reached added up to a solid foundation for cooperation.

Despite language barriers, Channa believed that problems could be solved as long as both parties tried their best to understand each other. "The greatest contributor to the partnership was our daily dinner meeting, which gave us ample opportunities to share ideas related to the overall plan and the nuts and bolts of the documentary. It's when our thoughts collided and sparked that we began to understand each other's culture in a deep way. Of course, delicious Chinese food provided a powerful source of energy and made it easier for us to stand up to challenges," Channa said.

Yan Dong cited patience, consensus based on differences and being detail-orientated as keys to success working with foreign partners. In his eyes, there's no such thing as a Chinese proposal or foreign proposal. "Our final proposals are always proposals of the team," he said.

While discussing the outline of the documentary, Kenny suggested that environmental protection be treated as a priority, given the fact that the Bridge had to pass through the National Natural Reserve of Chinese White Dolphins. However, some members of the team did not see eye to eye on that, arguing that the Bridge had sufficient technological highlights to show off. Kenny's rationale was that the Western audience had a special concern for environmental protection issues.

Yan supported Kenny. In his view, "Made in China" is not just about meeting hardcore engineering and technical standards, but also embodies concepts of sustainable development and ecological conservation. "The Chinese people are becoming increasingly aware of the importance of environmental protection. Both parties value sustainable development," Yan said.

As it turned out, citing the case of the eco-friendly Temburong Bridge in Brunei that China has helped build, the documentary illustrates how designers, engineers and builders of the Hong Kong-Zhuhai-Macao Bridge have taken environmental protection measures to minimize the potential adverse impact of the project on the National Natural Reserve of Chinese White Dolphins. Consequently, the concept of sustainable development featuring a harmonious relationship between humanity and nature got fully and vividly exemplified, thus providing a perfect answer to the question why "Made in China" could find its way out of the country and into the world.

After numerous discussions, the parties came to a consensus that the end product should be more than a documentary of a mega engineering project. But the challenge of beating the monotony and complexities of covering a civil engineering project was real. What's the best and wisest way to deal with a rigid subject matter so that the audience might find it engaging? This was the test Yan Dong and his coworkers had to go through.

"After the past two decades or so, Americans or Europeans have reconciled themselves to the fact that the Chinese people can work wonders. So their curiosity is now tilted more toward the people behind the mega project," Kenny suggested, "What I wanted to tell my Western friends was that the Chinese people building the Bridge are no different from Westerners. They each have emotions of their own, personalities of their own, dreams of their own, and ideas of their own."

Kenny found the scene of a young couple taking their pre-wedding photos on the Bridge delightful because, as builders of the mega project, they were demonstrating attachment to their workplace. The human touch brought life and feelings to the Bridge.

"After watching the documentary, what you remember might be the stories of Jing Qiang, Lin Ming, Wen Hua and Sun Hongchun, but add them together, you would have a story of the Bridge and a story of China in general. What the Bridge speaks of is the creativity of the people and the comprehensive power of the state," Yan said.

Channa agreed with that. "It represents the Chinese people's determination in solving infrastructure facilities issues. Brave Chinese workers and engineers dedicated their best years to making this grand project a reality. The documentary focuses on showcasing their will power," Channa stressed.

Discussion about the production of the documentary *The Hong Kong-Zhuhai-Macao Bridge*

Cultural Connotations

Yan has been thinking about shooting a documentary on Chinese bridges ever since he entered the movie and television industry. His first coverage of bridges, for example, can be found in his maiden work – a documentary entitled *Chinese Vernacular Dwellings*. "Bridges are icons of Chinese wisdom, adventurism, romanticism, and aestheticism, and an important part of Chinese culture," Yan said, "China's rich cultural tradition and experience in bridge-building accumulated since ancient times are crucial elements that make the Hong Kong-Zhuhai-Macao Bridge possible."

Kenny shared Yan's insight interpreting the Bridge from the perspective of Chinese culture. For the past decade, Kenny has focused on working on themes related to China. He filmed *China from Above* for National Geographic Channel, documentaries on the Cao Cao Museum of Western Han Dynasty and *Mausoleum of Nanyue King in Guangzhou* for History Channel and a series of other works about China for Discovery Channel.

Kenny pointed out that the documentary's use of "pearls" and "jade" to refer to the integrated culture embodied in the Bridge had cultural connotations because pearls and jade carried implications of purity and perfection in Chinese culture.

Yan said that part of the reason he could tap deep into the depository of Chinese culture and find all kinds of treasure was that he had spent 12 years working consistently on *The Chinese Memory*, a documentary on the preservation of China's cultural heritage.

A Bridge of Communication

Bridges existed in the first place primarily to meet humanity's needs to connect and communicate with the outside world. The purpose of Hong Kong-Zhuhai-Macao Bridge across one of the world's busiest waterways is to connect some of the world's most economically dynamic regions and make life easier for people living across these regions. However, Yan and his crew not only saw the Bridge as China's link with the world but also saw their documentary as a bridge of communication because it would help Westerners better understand China.

The Documentary Movie

Success of the TV documentary gave Yan Dong the drive to convert it into a documentary movie. The movie casts the image of a nation constantly striving to improve itself as it goes about fulfilling the Chinese Dream while tracking the miracles the Bridge has created from a historical perspective. A review of China's bridge-building history can help young people derive a sense of a cultural identity and national pride, Yan said.

Compared with the TV version, the movie focuses more on builders of the Bridge than the Bridge itself. Chief Engineer Lin Ming in charge of the artificial islands and the tunnel work is one of the main characters. Yan sees Lin as a wise, brave, determined, patient and tolerant person ready to take on challenges and responsibilities. "He used the pertinent parable of an intern driver without the guidance of an experienced one to describe the awkward situation he found himself in when construction

A section of the Hong Kong-Zhuhai-Macao Bridge

of the Bridge got started. What he's been through throughout the years is all reflected in the shadow of his figure standing alone on the deck," Yan said. Lin and his team failed twice trying to sink E15 immersed tubes (undersea tunnels in prefabricated segments) into place and had to go through twists and turns before eventually succeeding in installing E30, the last immersed tube. By documenting the process, the movie shows how persistence and perseverance have led to the miraculous success of the Hong Kong-Zhuhai-Macao Bridge, Yan said during an interview.

Yan Dong thinks that all builders of the Bridge, regardless of their job descriptions, reflect the spirit and character of the Chinese nation and endow the Bridge with a unique personality glamor. When asked to express their feelings about the Bridge they participated in building, a number of average builders simply chanted out: "I built the Hong Kong-Zhuhai-Macao Bridge!" "That's the voice of China," said Yan, who devised the unique ending.

Another point Yan Dong wanted to make with the movie is that the bridge reflects the change of fate of the Chinese

A member of the camera crew is shooting the
Hong Kong-Zhuhai-Macao Bridge

people, as reflected in the gripping story of Mao Yisheng, a bridge guru and an idol of Yan.

In the 1930s, after overcoming more than 80 technical problems, Mao Yisheng and his civil engineering team succeeded in building the Qiantang River Bridge, a 1,453-meter-long and 71-meter-high dual-purpose road-and-railway bridge, the first of its kind ever designed and built by a Chinese. Nonetheless, Mao did not hesitate to destroy the bridge for effective resistance against Japanese aggression. "He purposely designed a storage space in the bridge to hoard explosives and witnessed the entire detonation process," the narrator says in the documentary. In an ironic twist, construction and destruction of the bridge were both acts of patriotism. The moral of the story is that, while a poor and weak China of the past could not keep what it had built, a strong and prosperous China today can build the world's longest cross-sea bridge.

Overall, in the process of documenting how a cutting-edge sea bridge is made, the movie breathes life into a humongous object of technology and steel and concrete by telling touching human interest stories. The artistic and commercial success of the movie indicates that mainstream-theme Chinese documentaries are beginning to win worldwide recognition.

The Hong Kong-Zhuhai-Macao Bridge production team

A section of the Hong Kong-Zhuhai-Macao Bridge

Appendix I

Creators of the Documentary
The Hong Kong-Zhuhai-Macao Bridge

Chief Planners
ZHANG NING   ZHANG HUIJIAN   WEI DONGQING   FANG QI

Chief Supervisors
KAN ZHAOJIANG   ZHANG FANG
CHEN YIZHU   SHI YANFENG

Supervisors
ZHANG GUANGYI   GUO LIN
LI HONGRONG   VIKRAM CHANNA

General Producer
YAN DONG

Producers
LING QINGJIAN   BAI LI   ZHENG YUANJUN
HOU ZHANZONG   CHEN XIAOJUN

Director
YAN DONG

Executive Directors
KENNY PNG   LI KAI

Script
KENNY PNG   YAN JINGMING   DENG WU

Executive Producers
ZHANG YUANCONG   XUE YONGKANG   LI KAI

DENG WU   NIE CONGCONG

Assistant Directors
DIXIE CHAN   ZHANG YIZAI   LIU XIAORONG
ZHANG HAO   WU SHENGLI   SAM   JIANG WEI

Camera
JAYE NEO   WANGHONGJIANG   ZHU XUEFENG
ZHANG HANCHONG   ZHANG KANNING   ALBERT HUE
WU HAITAO   WANG CHUNTIAN   XIONG XIANGKUN

Translators
LU XING   GUI JIA   TORD SVENDSEN   LOEVDAL

Narrator
FANG LIANG

Music Editor
MAO WEIWEI

Aerial Photography
ZHANG HAO   ZHAO LINJUN   ZHA JUN
SONG CHEN   LU RUI

Camera Assistants
MA DI   CHEN YONGHAO   ZHENG ZHIMING
ZHAO BO   DU WEI

Technical Directors
ZHI WEI   CUI JIANWEI

Technical Supervisors
LI XIAOBIN   YAO PING   DAN JING
GUAN CHAOYANG   LIU RU

Sound Mixing
HE FENG   ZHANG SHUANG   WANG LAN

Copyright

ZHENG ZHI YAN BO XU TAO
HUANG FANG DA HONG

Programme Design

HONG LIJUAN WANG LIHUAN ZHANG DEHONG
QIN YI ZHANG XUEMIN ZHAI HUAN

Publicity

CHEN ZHONG GUO WEIXIANG
YUAN WENGANG ZHAO JUNSHENG

Promotion

ZHAO JINGJIN LIUMINGHUANG LIJUN LI JINHUA
PEI NING SHI YAN TIAN CHUYUN SUN LIANLIAN
ZHU HONGZHAN ZHANG LAN DUAN XIAOCHEN

News Media Supervisors

QIAN WEI LUO QIN JIN YANLIN
SONG WEIJUN WEI QUHU

News Media

ZHAO JUNSHENG WANG JINGDONG
SU CHUNLI ZHANG LI
XING MING LIU LIANG TIAN HONG WANG YUXI
LIU ZHEN CHANG LEI ZHANG JING ZHANG XIJIAN
SUN JING LIANG BINGXUE HU YUE ZHAO WEN
ZHANG YANLI DONG JIUGE

Post-production

WU YANG SU JIAO LIU TIANYU
WANG KAI HUANG JI

Post-production Design

SUN KAI LI YI

Archive Supervisor
NI DAIGUANG

Archive Editors
HAN XUEQIAO   PAN TENG   LI ZHIYUAN   ZHANG RAN

Visual Design
JIANG TAO

Production Managers
WANG JIANTONG   HAN ZHONGPENG   QIU WENHUI

Producers
TANG LIJUAN   WANG AIAI   GUO ZHIYONG
GONG JUAN   GE RENHAI

With Special Thanks to
Bureau of Publicity, State-owned Assets Supervision and Administration
Commission of the State Council

Published and Distributed by
China International Television Corporation

Book Version Published and Distributed by
China International Publishing Group
New World Press

Co-produced by
CCTV-Education
HKZM Bridge Administration
Discovery Networks Asia-Pacific
Guangdong TV
Zhuhai TV

June 2017

Appendix II

Participants of Main Work of the Hong Kong-Zhuhai-Macao Bridge Project

I. Preliminary Design

China Highway Planning and Design Institute Inc.

COWI A/S

Ove Arup & Partners Hong Kong Ltd

Shanghai Tunnel Engineering & Rail Transit Design and Research Institute

CCCC First Harbour Consultants Co Ltd

II. Design and Construction Consulting

Shanghai Municipal Engineering Design Institute Co., Ltd. (Leader)

T.Y.LIN International Group Limited

Holland Tunnel Engineering Consultant

Guangzhou Metro Design & Research Institute Co., Ltd.

III. Quality Management Consultancy of the HZMB Main Work

Mott MacDonald Co., Ltd.

Mott MacDonald Consultancy Co., Ltd (Beijing).

IV. General Contractors of Design and Construction of the Artificial Islands and Tunnel

China Communications Construction Co. (Leader)

China Highway Planning and Design Institute Inc.

AECOM Asia Company Ltd.,

COWI A/S

Shanghai Urban Construction (Group) Co.

Shanghai Tunnel Engineering & Rail Transit Design and Research Institute

CCCC Fourth Harbor Engineering Investigation and Design Institute

V. Supervisors of Artificial Islands and Tunnel

China Railway Wuhan Bridge Engineering Consultation & Management Co., Ltd. (Leader)

Guangzhou Port & Waterway Engineering Supervision Company

Guangzhou Municipal Engineering Supervision Co., Ltd.

VI. Bridge Construction Drawing Design of HZMB Main Work (DB01 section)

CCCC Highway Consultants Co., Ltd (Leader)

Chodai Co., LTD., JAPAN

VII. Bridge Construction Drawing Design of HZMB Main Work (DB02 section)

China Railway Bridge Survey & Design Institute Co., Ltd. (Organizer)

Halcrow Group Limited

VIII. Procurement and Manufacturing of Steel Box Girders for Bridge Construction (CB01 Section)

China Railway Shanhaiguan Bridge Group Co., Ltd.

IX. Procurement and Manufacturing of Steel Box Girders for Bridge Construction (CB02 Section)

Wuchang Shipbuilding Industry Group Co., Ltd.

X. Bridge Construction and Civil Construction (CB03 Section)

CCCC First Harbour Engineering Company Ltd. (Organizer)

CCCC Second Highway Engineering Co., Ltd.

XI. Bridge Construction and Civil Construction (CB04 Section)

Guangdong Provincial Changda Highway Engineering Co., Ltd.

XII. Bridge Construction, Civil Construction and Composite Beam Construction (CB05 Section)

China Railway Major Bridge Engineering Group Co., Ltd.

XIII. Bridge Deck Pavement (CB06 Section)

Chongqing Zhi Xiang Paving Technology Engineering Co., Ltd.

XIV. Bridge Deck Pavement (CB07 Section)
Guangdong Provincial Changda Highway Engineering Co., Ltd.

XV. Supervision of Manufacturing Steel Box Girders for Bridge Construction (SB01 Section)
China Classification Society Industrial Corp.

XVI. Supervision of Manufacturing Steel Box Girders for Bridge Construction (SB02 Section)
Wuhan Bridge and Building Works Supervision Co., Ltd.

XVII. Supervision of Bridge Construction and Civil Construction (SB03 Section)
Hubei Supervision Company of China Railway Siyuan Survey and Design Group Co., Ltd. (Leader)
Guangzhou Nanhua Project Management Co., Ltd.

XVIII. Supervision of Bridge Construction and Civil Construction (SB04 Section)
Xi'an Fangzhou Engineering Consulting Co., Ltd. (Leader)
China Classification Society Industrial Corp.

XIX. Supervision of Bridge Construction and Bridge Deck Pavement (SB05 Section)
Xi'an Fangzhou Engineering Consulting Co., Ltd.

XX. Test Center of the HZMB Main Work
Guangdong Hualu Traffic Technology Co., Ltd. (Organizer)
Jiangsu Transportation Research Institute Co. Ltd.

XXI. Measurement and Control Center of the HZMB Main Work
China Railway Bridge Survey & Design Institute Co., Ltd. (Organizer)
XXII. Third-Party Testing of Steel Box Girders, Composite Beams, and Steel Cable Towers for Bridge Construction

Jiangsu Fasten Group Co., Ltd.

XXIII. Transport Project Drawing Design
Jiaoke Transport Consultancy Ltd.

XXIV. Transport Project Construction (CA02 Section)
China Railway Construction Electrification Bureau Group Co., Ltd.
(Leader)
The First Engineering Co., Ltd. of China Railway Construction
Electrification Bureau Group

XXV. Supervision of Transport Project Construction (SA02 Section)
Chongqing Zhongyu Consultation & Supervision Co., Ltd. (Leader)
Zhuhai Power Project Supervision Co., Ltd.

XXVI. Housing Construction Project Drawing Design
Architectural Design and Research Institute of Guangdong Province

XXVII. Housing Construction Project (CA01 Section)
Hunan Construction Engineering Group

XXVIII. Supervision of Housing Construction Project (SA01 Section)
Guangdong Zhonggong Project Management Co., Ltd.

XXIX. Bridge Test Pile Construction and Experimental Investigation
Guangdong Provincial Changda Highway Engineering Co., Ltd. (Leader)
Highway Research Institute of Ministry of Transport

XXX. Full-scale Model Test of Embedded Bearing Platforms for the
HZMB Main Work
CCCC Second Harbour Engineering Company Ltd.

XXXI. Integrated Information System Development of the HZMB Main
Work
Phase One Guangdong Oriental Thought Technology Co., Ltd.
Phase Two Guangdong TOONE Technology Co., Ltd.

Postscript

On August 5, 2018, an award ceremony in honor of Exceptional Domestic Documentaries and Emerging Talent Support Programs for 2017 was held in BTV Theater in Beijing. The Exceptional International Communication Award in the documentary category went to *The Hong Kong-Zhuhai-Macao Bridge*. This was the fourth prize the TV documentary fetched in 2017. The documentary in two episodes (a total of 100 minutes) was directed by Yan Dong and co-produced by CCTV-10 (the science and education channel), the Hong Kong-Zhuhai-Macao Bridge Authority, Discovery Channel, Guangdong Radio & Television (GRT) and Zhuhai Radio and Television (ZHTV).

For more than eight years, CCTV, GRT and ZHTV worked closely in partnership. With full support from the Hong Kong-Zhuhai-Macao Bridge Authority, the production team spent innumerable sleepless nights with the builders at all critical stages of the construction project, documenting their outstanding performance and sharing their weal and woe.

On June 30 and July 1, 2017, the TV documentary was broadcast successively on CCTV-10, CCTV-1 and CGTN. In the meantime, it was distributed and disseminated to nearly 450 million viewers through various terminals of CCTV.com and was hit and/or watched for more than 37.54 million times. It was applauded highly by netizens all over the world. Soon after that, it was aired on Discovery Channel as well. *Wen Yi Bao* published a news commentary referring to the documentary as "a homage to the project of the century" that "helps boost China's national strategy." The news bureau of the CPC Central Committee's Publicity Department stated in its newsletter that the documentary ignited the audience's patriotism and served as a tribute for the 20th anniversary of Hong Kong's return to China.

Instead of being carried away by the accolades received, the production team led by Yan Dong went on board a new voyage of hard work, during which they dug deep into their source materials, reorganized them and reproduced it into a documentary movie that differed completely from the TV version. The 75-minute movie, which took a year to complete, is also called *The Hong Kong-Zhuhai-Macao Bridge*. While the TV documentary presents, in a kaleidoscopic style, the design philosophy, building process, and main body of the Bridge including the artificial islands and undersea tunnel, the movie version adopts a lineal structure, highlighting human elements, story-telling, and intricate character portrayal.

During production of both versions, the team received strong support and great advice from authorities of the State Film Administration, the State Council's State-owned Assets Supervision and Administration Commission (SASAC), and the Ministry of Transport. When the movie was done, China Film Co., Ltd chose its best team to market and distribute the movie.

Since 2004, New World Press has published a number of books adapted from Yan Dong's documentaries, including *Main Battlefield in the East, Memories of Nanjing 1937, Confucius, The Long March, Deng Xiaoping:1904-2004*. These books, mostly published in Chinese, English, Japanese, Russian and French, have been exhibited at a series of international book fairs, including Frankfurt Book Fair, London Book Fair, New York Book Fair, Beijing International Book Fair and India Book Fair, and have received positive comments from readers all over the world. *Main Battlefield in the East* won the Overseas Publicity Book Award for 2016 from China International Publishing Group (CIPG).

With funding support from CIPG, *The Hong Kong-Zhuhai-Macao Bridge* is being published by New World Press in Chinese, English and Portuguese so that more people from across the world will have a better idea of the Bridge, of China's latest achievements in construction and of the spiritual status of Chinese builders. We hereby dedicate this book to builders of the Hong Kong-Zhuhai-Macao Bridge.

The Hong Kong-Zhuhai-Macao Bridge Production Team
August 2018

图书在版编目（CIP）数据

港珠澳大桥：英文 /《港珠澳大桥》纪录片摄制组
著；陆星等译 . -- 北京：新世界出版社，2019.6
ISBN 978-7-5104-6682-3

Ⅰ . ①港… Ⅱ . ①港… ②陆… Ⅲ . ①跨海峡桥—桥
梁工程—概况—中国—英文 Ⅳ . ① U448.19

中国版本图书馆 CIP 数据核字 (2018) 第 284820 号

港珠澳大桥（英文）

作　　者：《港珠澳大桥》纪录片摄制组
翻　　译：陆　星　桂　嘉　Tord Svendsen Loevdal　于　泓　江　曦
责任编辑：闫传海　孔德芳
装帧设计：贺玉婷
排版设计：魏芳芳
责任印制：王宝根　苏爱玲
出版发行：新世界出版社
社　址：北京西城区百万庄大街 24 号（100037）
发 行 部：(010) 6899 5968 (010) 6899 8705（传真）
总 编 室：(010) 6899 5424 (010) 6832 6679（传真）
http://www.nwp.cn http://www.nwp.com.cn
版 权 部：+8610 6899 6306
版权部电子信箱：nwpcd@sina.com
印　刷：北京京华虎彩印刷有限公司
经　销：新华书店
开　本：710mm×1000mm 1/16
字　数：200 千字
印　张：12.5
版　次：2019 年 6 月第 1 版　2019 年 6 月北京第 1 次印刷
书　号：ISBN 978-7-5104-6682-3
定　价：98.00 元